Sometimes what you know to be the truth is nothing but an elaborate lie.

Azilia's life is turned upside down when her grandmother leaves her an old antique shop in her will, forcing her to run the musty old store for two years or lose her inheritance.

Reluctant to accept her inheritance, she is given a letter written by her grandmother that changes the stakes—and Azilia's life forever.

Antique Trove
Copyright © 2019 Taryn Jameson and Gabriella Bradley
ISBN: 978-1-4874-2471-8
Cover art by Martine Jardin

Look for us online at:
www.eXtasybooks.com or
www.devinedestinies.com

Antique Trove

By

Taryn Jameson and
Gabriella Bradley

To our readers!

CHAPTER ONE

Azilia glared at the elderly lawyer behind his antique desk. "Damn it! I will *not* do it! I am Chief Engineer of the spaceship *Cepheus*. We are leaving tomorrow on an urgent mission." Her Earth father's language had filtered into hers, as it had with her brothers and sisters. The timing of the mission had disappointed her because she would miss Christmas, but she had no choice.

"The captain has already been informed that you will not be returning to duty for two years due to family matters."

"How *dare* you!" Azilia tilted her chin in

1

defiance, ready to spit venom about what the lawyer had just told her. "You do *not* have that right!"

He adjusted his glasses on his face and gave her a blank stare. "I discussed the situation with the council, and it was their decision to inform your superiors, not mine. Your grandmother's last wishes are very clear. You are to operate her antique shop for two years, or you will forfeit the inheritance."

"Then I will forfeit, and I will leave anyway. If the Royal Space Corps will not take me back because of this, I am sure I can find another outbound private enterprise that will employ me," Azilia said stubbornly.

She noticed old Ogwon was becoming quite agitated. His fingers visibly shook as he picked up a tablet, punched in a code and shoved it toward her. She felt sorry for him in a way. She had known the old lawyer her whole life. He had been her family's lawyer for many generations and seemed to outlive them all. Giving him such a hard time was unfair because he was merely following her grandmother's last instructions and doing his job.

"This letter was sealed by your grandmother so that only you could view it. Activate it with your thumbprint and then read it," Ogwon ordered in a somewhat shaky voice.

Reluctantly, she picked up the tablet, and after placing her thumb on the designated spot. Her vision became blurry as she looked at her grandmother's letter. She swallowed hard trying to clear the lump in her throat.

For all her bravado, she had loved her grandmother more than any of her other family members, even her parents. There was a closeness, a connection between them that she did not have with any of the others, not even her mother.

Why did Groma have to die so soon? The Pazonans lived for many generations. Why not her grandmother? She choked up at the thought of the childhood nickname for her grandmother that had stuck throughout the years. When she could not pronounce grandmother, she had come up with Groma.

Why did Groma have to contract the feared blood disease that struck one in a million, and for which there was no cure? No magic, no potions, nothing could fix it.

She took a deep breath and concentrated on the letter on the screen.

My sweet Azilia,

I have known for some time that I would be one to contract the Zigoni virus. I never told your mother, or anyone, because I did not know when it would strike. I am just thankful I have lived this long.

You, my darling girl, I favor over all my children, grandchildren, and great-grandchildren, and there is a reason for that. I am so proud of what you have accomplished, of the woman you have become, of conquering the obstacles you have encountered throughout your life. But there is another big reason.

As you know, you are different from your parents, your siblings, from me, and the rest of the family. You always have been the odd one out, and it caused you much grief during your growing years. The doctors called you an anomaly. I bribed them to tell your parents that. In all honesty, they had no clue.

In private, the doctor mentioned to me that it could be the mixed marriage, your father being from Earth. I didn't want them to tell your parents that either because it did not make sense. They had already brought twelve other normal healthy children into the world, and none of them displayed any abnormalities.

Ah, I am so much to blame there, and I hope you will take my secret to your grave with you. Your mother would never forgive me if she knew where you are really from.

I am leaving you my beloved Antique Trove. I want you to take care of it, run it, love it as I have for so many years. Later, with your career and space travels, you will be able to add so much more to my shop and expand it.

I am sure you will be able to manage running the shop and still keep your position as a chief engineer. I request and trust that you will never, ever sell it. I ask of you, if you must continue your space career, that you will employ someone to operate it.

I would like you to run the shop for two years. And right now, you are wondering why. And knowing my girl so well, you are angry and frustrated and probably taking it out on poor old Ogwon.

Twenty-six years ago, during my travels and hunt for antiques, I came upon a beautiful, ornate, antique golden metal chest inside an unexplored cave. It just stood there, apparently abandoned. But it was in such excellent condition I almost hesitated to take it. What if someone came back for it? Hidden inside the chest was an old clock that was somewhat broken. I had a feeling I had to take the chest, and as you know, my intuition is never wrong. When I got home later that night, I put the chest in the shop and went upstairs to bed.

That same night, several hours before sunrise, your mother came to me. She was not yet due to give birth to her thirteenth infant, and your father was away on one of his voyages. Your mother had waited too long to warn someone. She was in heavy labor, and it was too late to call the midwife, so I had to deliver the babe. The poor mite was born two months early and was stillborn. I did not yet have the heart to tell my poor Stabila, and I let her hold the baby girl. Through her exhausted state, she did not notice there was no life in the child. After she fell asleep, I took the infant from her arms and went downstairs to the shop. Not yet knowing what to do with the little one, I temporarily hid her in the chest.

The next morning your mother was still asleep when I went to open the shop. As I reached the base of the staircase, I heard the cries of an infant coming from the chest. I rushed to it, and lo and behold, there you were. I do not know what happened to the stillborn babe. She had disappeared.

I swaddled you and placed you in your mother's arms. Your strange appearance and odd hair color were blamed on your early birth. I blackmailed the physicians that ran tests on you into silence. They told your mother that having another child so late in life caused the anomaly.

You are not of our world, honey. I am sure of that.

The chest and the clock, well-hidden in the back of the shop, must hold the secrets of your heritage. It is important you keep them together. And now it is time for you to discover your roots. How? I do not know. I strongly believe the chest has the answers, or maybe the clock. Perhaps you can figure it out, and I hope two years is enough time for you to do that. Forgive me for not finding those answers, please? I fell in love with you the moment I saw you and could not bear the thought of losing such a precious gift.

Sweet girl, I love you and will always be with you in spirit.

Your loving grandmother.

An anomaly? Her beloved family was not truly her own? Azilia fought against the tears that threatened. After swallowing hard several times, she looked at Ogwon. "I need you to send this to my tablet, and you have to erase the letter from yours."

After reading her grandmother's letter, she knew she would keep the shop and obey her Groma's last wish. The thought of giving up her position on the ship for two years gnawed at her, but she really had no choice.

"All right, my dear, if that is what you wish. Now we need to discuss the takeover of the Antique Trove. There are documents for you to sign." He showed her his tablet as he sent the letter to her, then deleted it from his system. He brought up other documents.

In a daze, Azilia signed the necessary documents with her thumbprint.

"Your grandmother did not only leave you the shop, but she also left you a large amount of gold coin. If you tell me which bank you deal with and give me your account number, I will have it transferred into your account."

Azilia gave him her banking information and watched him complete the transaction, then he handed her the key to the shop. Sticking the key in her pocket and still feeling quite overwhelmed, she left the lawyer's office, mounted her hoverbike and set course for her small home.

Once inside her apartment, she made herself a pot of calming herbal tea, then sat on the couch and thought about what had just transpired. In one swift moment, her life had been turned completely upside down.

Her tablet pinged, pulling her out of deep thought. She clicked the answer button, and her mother appeared in the holograph that popped up.

"Honey? What did the lawyer say?"

"Grandmother left me her shop, Mother."

"What? Really. Why would she bypass her children?"

"I do not know, Mother. I am sure no one in the family wanted the old shop. No one but me has ever shown an interest in the antiques. Everyone else calls it junk." She did know one big reason of course why her grandmother had left her Antique Trove, but she could not tell her mother, or anyone else. What would she say? *Oh, Mother, by the way, I am not your child? I am some anomaly Grandmother found in an old chest?*

"You are probably right. And that old shop with all the junk it has in it would not be worth much on today's market anyway. She left the rest of her fortune to her children. I should not complain. It just surprises me."

"Yes. Like it surprised the hell out of me," Azilia muttered under her breath.

Her mother quickly switched topics to one of her favorites. "Zilly, you are twenty-six years old. When are you going to settle down? Your brothers and sisters are all married. It is time—"

"Mother. Stop already. And do not call me that. You know how I hate it. You know very well no man wants a misfit like me. Be happy I got the shop. Grandmother's will stipulates that I have to run the shop for two years straight, so you will see a lot more of me." Azilia wrinkled her nose. It was just like her mother to harp on about marriage and babies. Well, she was not like her brothers and sisters. Never had been, and now she knew the reason for it.

"For goodness sake, why? What about your job?"

"I will need to take a leave of absence, although, according to Ogwon, it has already been taken care of. I cannot sell the shop. I have no choice."

"Will you have to live in the house above the shop?"

"Yes, Mother. I will pack what I am taking

with me tonight and move to Antique Trove tomorrow morning. This place came furnished, so there really isn't much to pack."

"It just occurred to me. You were supposed to leave on another mission tomorrow. Now you will be home for Christmas." A broad smile brightened her mother's face. "Would you like me to come and help you pack?"

"Thanks, but there is no need. I had better get going. Goodnight, Mother."

"Rest well, Zilly." Her mother's image winked out, and the tablet screen went dark.

After drinking the rest of her tea, she stood and got down on her hands and knees, reached beneath her bed, and pulled out the two storage units she had used when moving in. Because of her travels, she had never amassed much during her time in the apartment—a few trinkets, some pictures and ornaments, and her clothes. She resolved to pack right there and then and would leave first thing in the morning.

Packing took her less than an hour.

Another soothing cup of tea later, she decided to shower and go to bed. But sleep would not come. Her grandmother's letter weighed heavy on her mind. Her parents were not truly her parents, her siblings not her real brothers and sisters. No wonder she looked so different from them. Her siblings were all a mix of Earthling and Pazonan.

Her father had been from Earth. She missed him so much, but unlike the people of Pazona, he did not have the luxury of an extended lifetime.

How had she ended up in the chest with that clock? How was it possible? Her grandmother had placed a dead infant in the chest. And somehow, during the night, the dead babe had disappeared, and Azilia had taken its place. It was all too crazy for words. Perhaps it was all a hallucination — the letter, the baby swap. Maybe she truly was merely an anomaly.

CHAPTER TWO

Azilia woke disoriented. She sat up and gazed at the two storage units in the middle of the room. She was not hallucinating. The nightmare was very real. She took a deep, shuddering breath and lay back down, hoping to sink into blissful oblivion. Instead, sleep eluded her. She was plagued with dreams about chests, clocks with arms and legs, and big mouths with sharp teeth that gobbled up babies and then spat them out again in bits and pieces.

Then there was the hotter than hell man. He was not new to her dreams, though. He had been her companion in her sleep so often over the years. She had no clue who he was. It was not anyone she had ever met. It would not have been so bad if he had entered her dreams just before she woke up, but it was the crazy chest and clock that had her waking up in a sweat that morning.

She vigorously rubbed her face, then jumped off the bed and ran to the bathroom to wash and brush her teeth. After raking a brush through her thick aqua and mauve hair, she gazed at her reflection. Yes, she was different. Not just the color of her hair, her facial features were missing the ridges all her family members had, some more pronounced than others—her siblings being half Earthling. Their hair was all shades of brown and black, and their skin olive colored or creamy. Her skin color was much lighter, and unlike her siblings, she had strange mauve and aqua colored shiny spots on her forehead and temples, down the sides of her neck, on her abdomen, and along her thighs. They reminded her of fish scales and often peeled off.

Her mother had tried salves, had taken her to doctors, and to the most powerful sorceress, Sadinia, on Pazona, but nothing helped. No one could cure the strange skin condition. She was the first to have been born with it on Pazona, and it had baffled doctors and specialists for years.

She sighed and climbed into her uniform. It was comfortable and covered most of her skin imperfections. Even if she had to work and live at the Antique Trove, there was no way she was going to start wearing dresses or skirts and blouses.

After sending her notice to her landlord, she gazed at the two cases and decided she should call for a minicab. She would pick up her bike later.

The minicab dropped Azilia off at the front entrance of Antique Trove. She fished the key from her pocket, unlocked the door, and hauled her cases into the shop, then up the stairs to the apartment above it. Her throat constricted for a moment as she stood in the familiar clutter of her grandmother's abode. As a child, she had loved investigating all the scattered treasures her grandmother had collected over the years. Some of them were from faraway places.

Growing up, she had loved listening to her grandmother's adventurous tales and her father's stories of his space travel and trading. They had both visited many planets and galaxies in the quest for trade and unique items for her grandmother's shop. Those stories were the reason Azilia had enrolled in the space academy. It was the one common denominator she had with two people in her family — and now even that commonality was shattered. She could not have inherited her adventurous nature from her grandmother or her father, because they were not related by blood.

Dragging the cases to the spare room, she almost threw them in there. Damn, they were heavy. She avoided her grandmother's bedroom. They were never allowed inside it as children unless Groma said it was okay, and if she entered it now, it would feel like she was invading her grandmother's privacy. It was stupid. Her grandmother was gone, but it still felt wrong.

After unpacking her cases and reducing their size to almost half, she pushed them under the bed. She hung her pictures on the walls, placed her ornaments in spots around the room, and adjusted some furniture here and there until the room almost felt like her own.

After she finished adjusting her room, she decided to head to the kitchen to find some food. But passing her grandmother's bedroom door, she could not help but open it and peek inside. Just for a moment, she imagined Groma sitting in the rocking chair near the fireplace. Occasionally, when she was small, Groma had allowed her in, set her on her lap, and would read her a story near a roaring fire. Fighting the emotions that wanted to surface, she closed the door and continued her quest for food.

The kitchen was exactly as her grandmother had left it. Death had come too swiftly. The dreaded disease had appeared, and within a day, Groma had slept in, never to wake again.

Stale, moldy bread sat on a plate on the counter. The kettle filled with herbal tea sat on the stove. Azilia chucked the bread in the garbage and put the plate in the sink. She emptied the kettle, filled it with fresh water, and set it on the burner. After searching through the cupboards, she found a package of biscuits. That would have to do for breakfast. She munched on them while she waited for the water to boil.

After sweetening her tea with hulna, a syrup her father used to call *honey*, she took her mug and went downstairs to investigate the shop. The closed sign was still up, so she would not be disturbed just yet. Not that Antique Trove was that busy, but people did come in to browse.

The chest. Where to look for it? She set her mug on a dusty cupboard and heaved a big sigh as she glanced around at the clutter of antiques spread across the shop. They were set up on tables and benches, on shelves, lying or standing on the floor, clocks and paintings hung on the walls. Things were scattered everywhere. It was hard to find a place to walk between the disorganized mess.

Where did her grandmother hide the damn thing? Azilia zigzagged through the maze of antiques to the very back of the shop where boxes were piled on top of each other and stacked haphazardly.

She had just turned twenty-six. Meaning she had at least twenty-six years of accumulated junk to go through, and probably many years before that. The chest could not be that small, not if it were big enough for an infant to fit inside it.

She began moving things around, coughing from the dust she disturbed. Many of the items she found were priceless and sure as heck not the junk her mother had called it. A lot of the antiques needed to be moved to the front of the shop. She was going to have a hell of a time sorting through the whole mess. How could customers even navigate through it all?

It was not until late in the day when she spotted an ornate chest beneath a pile of boxes. It looked ancient. Dusty, yes, and dulled from time, but when cleaned up, it could fetch a tidy sum. A pang of excitement filled her. It had to be the one her grandmother had found her in.

Azilia removed all the boxes until she got to the chest. Cautiously, holding her breath, afraid she would find a tiny skeleton inside, she lifted the lid and only saw the old clock her grandmother had mentioned. It was littered with cobwebs, dust, and dead insects, but thankfully no bones were inside, just the broken clock.

She sat on one of the boxes and gazed down at the timepiece. It looked so old, so worn and moldy. Standing up, she decided to pull the chest to the front of the shop and clean it. It was heavy. It appeared to be made of ornate gold and engraved with special symbols and etchings.

She managed to drag it to the front of the shop. "I do not care how heavy you are. I am going to get you cleaned up," she muttered under her breath.

She turned to get the cleaning supplies when she noticed, to her surprise, people were standing outside the door peering at her through the glass.

Azilia chewed her bottom lip and looked at the time, then hurried to the shop's door. Had she really spent the whole morning searching for the chest?

"I am so sorry. I forgot to open this morning. What can I do for you?" She held the door open while the potential customers stepped inside.

"I'm so glad you're finally open again. Why was the shop closed? Where is the old lady?" The woman brushed past her and began examining items on a shelf.

Azilia took a deep breath as the grief wash over her. A pain she was told would lessen over time, but at that moment she knew it was a wound that would never heal.

"That lady was my grandmother. She passed away a week ago."

"Oh, I'm so sorry. My condolences. I always loved dealing with her." The woman gave her a small smile. "Are you taking over the store?"

"Yes. I am cleaning up right now."

"It shows." The woman brushed her hand through her blonde hair and continued perusing the shop.

Oh, damn. I'm all dusty. Azilia grimaced and quickly tried to adjust her hair, then brushed some of the dust off her suit and yanked a cobweb from a stray lock of hair.

"Oh, Colin, I want this box!" the woman called out.

The woman was pointing at *Azilia's* chest. Azilia hurried to the couple. There was no way in hell she would let the woman have it. That box could hold the secret to her roots. "I am sorry. It is not for sale."

She studied the couple a moment. They were not from Pazona. They were travelers and resembled her father.

"Where are you from?" As if she did not know already. *Stupid question.* Many people from Earth visited Pazona. That was how her mother had met her father.

"We're from Earth." The man smiled at her.

Azilia stepped in front of the chest. "Ah. I brought this chest out to clean it. It is not for sale. I apologize for the inconvenience."

"Oh, baby, I want it," the woman wheedled while winding an arm around the man's neck.

"I'll pay you two thousand gold grenots for it." He pulled a wallet from his suit pocket.

Oh, hell. That was quite a sum, but there was no way she could sell it. Not after what Groma had told her in the letter.

She shook her head. "Sorry, as I told you, it is not for sale."

"Then why is it here?" The woman pouted.

"I was in the process of cleaning and restoring it."

"And fixing the clock?" the man asked, pointing inside the chest. "Maybe you will sell it to us when you're finished with it?"

"Yes, I will repair the clock, and no, I will never sell it."

"It would be the perfect Christmas gift for my

mother," the woman continued to wheedle. "Just the chest. You can keep the clock." She wrinkled her nose. "It's badly broken anyway. I doubt you can fix it."

"Honey, the young lady doesn't want to sell it. You'll need to find something else."

"You know how Mother loves antiques."

The man became impatient. "Make up your mind. Are you going to find something here or do we go somewhere else? It's almost Christmas, for God's sake."

"I saw some other chests in the back. If you give me a few minutes, I can see if there is one you may like?" Azilia offered.

The woman had a porcelain statue in her hands. "Sure, I'll look around while we wait. I'll take this statue." She placed the graceful little ballerina on the counter. "By the way, I love the colors of your hair. Who is your hairdresser?"

Azilia almost burst out laughing. What would the woman say if she told her she was born that way? "I did it myself. I will go and look for another trunk for you now."

Azilia went to the back of the shop, swiping at cobwebs and sneezing from the disturbed dust. It was going to be a hellish job to clean it all and discover what was hidden under all that dust and what was in the many boxes.

Many smaller items stood loosely among

everything else. She spotted a snow globe with a Christmas scene inside. It was something her father had brought from Earth and given to her grandmother. *Christmas.* Because of her father, they celebrated it every year, though it was not a tradition on Pazona. But many people from Earth who had settled on Pazona visited Antique Trove and shopped for unique items to give as gifts.

The people of Pazona worshipped several gods and goddesses, but her father had always sworn there was only one God, and His son, Jesus, whose birthday was celebrated at Christmas. She had an interesting life, growing up with a mix of Earth's culture and Pazona's traditions and celebrations.

She found a wooden chest hidden in a corner. She used a cloth to wipe some of the dust from the wood. The chest was carved beautifully with a floral pattern and fairies, and the fine grain of the wood shone with a golden hue. The workmanship had been so finely detailed, Azilia knew it had to have been carved by a master of the craft.

"I found a gorgeous wooden chest that I think will interest you," she called out. "I'll bring it out to the front."

After she removed the boxes stacked on top of the chest, she pulled it out by one of its handles. It was too heavy to lift, so she dragged it to the front of the shop.

"Oooh, Mom will love it," the woman exclaimed. "Can you have it cleaned up and ready for me before you close tonight?"

"How much?" her husband asked.

Lord, how much? Azilia had no clue. Did her grandmother even have a price for it? She had to have kept records somewhere. "Twelve-hundred gold grenots. As you can see, it is hand-carved. And an extra five-hundred silver dranos for cleaning and polishing it."

"Do you know where it's from?" the man wanted to know.

"I would have to look up its record. I am sorry. It is my first day in the shop, so—"

"Don't worry about it. You can tell us later. My wife and her mother shop here all the time. I'm Colin Edgewater by the way, and this is my wife, Ellen. My wife's parents live on Pazona, in this town. We are here for the Christmas holidays," Colin said.

"You've got quite a task ahead of you to sort through the old lady's stuff," Ellen told her. "Come, honey. We have more shopping to do."

"Enjoy your holiday. Give me two hours, and I will have the chest ready for you." Azilia walked them to the door.

The couple left, and Azilia hunted for

supplies to begin the task of cleaning the chest. Her first sale and it was a good one. The guy had not even flinched at the price.

Not only did she have to get the chest ready, but it suddenly struck her that she was going to be home for Christmas and she had not bought one gift.

She had just returned from a mission, and on the same day she had found her grandmother so very ill, then her passing and the funeral. She had not had the time to even think about Christmas before her life had been turned upside down. And hell, their family was huge. Twelve brothers and sisters, their spouses, then there were all the nieces and nephews.

Azilia was the youngest child and the only one not married. That fact seemed to bother her siblings, and especially her mother. They often tried to pair her off with someone between her missions.

Blind dates are what her father had called them. There had been a number of them, even with men from other planets. Sadly, her skin condition turned them off. She knew that for a fact by comments and reactions. The only reason Azilia had even gone on the dates was to please her family.

Azilia had no desire for a man in her life, even less to have children. She quite enjoyed her nieces and nephews, and what was great, she could love them for a little while and then hand them back to their parents. No, once she got through the required two years in this shop, it was her goal to one day captain a ship of her own.

While she polished and rubbed, she made plans to take some evening courses at the science academy during her two-year stint in the shop.

When the chest was finished, Azilia put the lid back on the bottle of oil, picked up all the rags she had used, and stood back to inspect the finished product. The result was remarkable. She had no doubt that the Edgewaters would be pleased with the transformation.

"Perfect. I might as well hunt around for some Christmas gifts while I wait for them to pick it up," she said aloud.

Lord, she was turning into her grandmother. Every Christmas, Groma gave them all small gifts from her shop.

Azilia grimaced. No one could blame her for doing the same. She hardly had time now to go shopping. Tomorrow was Christmas Eve. Though her father was gone, in honor of his memory, her mother had continued the Christmas tradition he had started, but also because it brought the entire family together on

Christmas Day, the only time of the year when they were almost all under one roof. Azilia had not missed that many, but there were a few years when she had been in space, as she should have been again this time. But thanks to the inheritance from her grandmother, there should not be anyone missing this year.

She stopped to look at the selection of antique dolls and did a mental headcount of all her nieces. Except for the youngest, still a baby, the dolls would take care of the girls. Now what to give the boys? And her sisters and brothers? Her mother? Money was not an option. Mother had forbidden all of them to give monetary gifts. She loved the huge pile of presents under the tree, and the joy of watching her children and grandchildren opening them all.

The tree. Her father had brought it back with him after he and her mother got married and one of his missions had taken him to Earth. It was a fake tree, but it looked very real, and it even smelled real. It was so tall that it almost touched the high ceiling. There was just enough room left for the Christmas angel her father had brought with him to sit on top. And each time his travels took him to Earth, he brought back tons of Christmas decorations for inside the mansion, and for the grounds.

Now that Father was gone, her brothers

decorated her parents' huge house with lights and set up the Christmas display on the front lawn—a life-size Santa Claus in a sleigh with eight reindeer and several fake fully decorated Christmas trees. There were also candy canes, elf dolls that were the size of a child, and a little gingerbread house. They, too, were lit up with bright colored lights. Their house was quite an attraction at that time of the year, and people came from afar to admire it.

She found a huge box filled with colorful balls of all sizes. Okay, those would do for some of the nephews, but she would need to find something different for the older boys. After going through about ten boxes, she found one that had games in it. By the looks of them, they were from other planets. *Great.* That would keep the older nephews busy trying to figure the games out.

By the time the couple returned for their purchases, she had a gift for everyone except her mother.

"The chest is perfect," Ellen Edgewater exclaimed. "How much for the little statue?"

"Four hundred gold grenots." The little ballerina was very pretty, super fragile, but Azilia had no idea. She was running blind until she could look for records that evening. There had to be ledgers somewhere. Groma was old-fashioned. She did not like modern technology, so she still used pen and paper. Azilia thought she could be overcharging. What if the statue was not worth that much?

"Sold. That is a total of sixteen-hundred gold grenots and five-hundred silver dranos." Ellen smiled, then turned to her husband. "Colin, I will pay while you take the chest to the car."

The couple did not bat an eyelid at the price. It was a good thing Azilia had sometimes helped her grandmother when she was young, so she knew how to work the transaction. She quickly punched in the numbers on the transaction tablet, the only bit of modern technology Groma had bought, then handed it to Ellen to finalize it. "Thank you and have a Merry Christmas," she said while handing the wrapped statuette to her customer.

After they were gone, she hung the *closed* sign and locked the door. The day was nearly over anyway. She went upstairs to hunt for food. Another thing she needed to do. Go grocery shopping. Her grandmother's cooler was nearly empty. Her mother must have emptied it because Groma always had her cooler stocked. Azilia decided she would stock up after Christmas. She could live another day on canned and frozen foods.

After devouring a can of meat and a can of

mikkel beans, she grabbed a bottle of wine, a glass, and went back down to the shop. The gold chest still stood in the walkway. She knew if she shoved it underneath something, she would put off the task of cleaning it. Deciding to look for her grandmother's record ledgers later, she concentrated on the work of restoring and polishing the chest.

She took the clock out and carefully put it in a small box. Looking at the loose parts, gears, and small screws, she knew she could fix it easily. She was an engineer, after all.

The worst task was cleaning the chest. She fetched the small vacuum from under the counter, grabbed the cleaning supplies, and got to work.

A few hours later, it was finished. Azilia stood back and admired it. Now that it was polished, it really was a thing of beauty. It gleamed and sparkled in the soft lights of the shop. The etchings on it were foreign, engraved in intricate patterns she did not recognize. She wondered where it came from and who had abandoned it inside the cave.

After opening the bottle of wine and filling her glass, she sat on the high stool behind the counter and began working on the clock. The task was complex, requiring a steady hand and the utmost precision. It was close to midnight when she finally finished, and the clock in her hands ticked merrily. She set the time to three minutes before twelve and lifting it carefully, placed it back in the chest.

Azilia filled her glass again, took a few sips, then sat cross-legged on the floor in front of the chest. "Stupid really, to have a working clock inside a chest," she muttered. "Maybe I will give it to Mother for Christmas."

How the chest and the clock could help her figure out where she was from, assist her in discovering her roots, was beyond her comprehension.

Several of the antique clocks hanging on the walls began to chime, announcing midnight. Leaning on the chest, Azilia stood and began to lower the lid when something sizzled, and she felt an electric charge surge up her arm, then through her body. The outside of the chest glowed eerily, and the inside of it lit up with a brilliant orange and yellow colored light that grew into a large oval, the face of the clock reflected inside it. Startled, she yanked her hand back as if scalded.

"What in blazes is going—"

She got no further. A strong pull forced her to lift her foot, drew her into the chest, smack dab in the middle of the oval of light and face of the clock. Dizziness overwhelmed her, and her head throbbed with pain. The beat of her heart echoed in her ears as it threatened to jump out of her chest. She closed her eyes when the light flared as bright as a supernova.

CHAPTER THREE

It felt like hours had passed when the pounding of her heart finally simmered to a steady beat. She dared to open her eyes again and screamed. Directly in front of her stood an enormous reptile with wings. With a snap of its jaws, it lowered its head and glared at her. *What the hell? Is that a dragon? This is not happening.*

Dazed, she began to climb out of the chest. If she stepped clear, she would be back in her grandmother's shop, right?

"This is a dream. It is not real," Azilia muttered.

"This is no dream," the dragon said.

She must have lost her damn mind. Even though she was out of the chest, the hallucination was still there. She held her hands, palms out, in front of her body and took a careful step back. The last thing she wanted was to be this creature's lunch. "Okay. Now I know for sure I am dreaming or going crazy. Talking dragons?"

"You have finally come home," the dragon spoke again.

"Home?" *Oh, my God. I am actually answering the beast.*

She calmed down a bit. The dragon did not seem as if he wanted to gobble her up. It was actually quite beautiful with its shiny blue, purple, and red scales. But in all honesty? A talking dragon? And where in the gods' names was she? *This is just another one of my stupid nightmares.*

"No nightmare. I assure you I am very real."

Her eyes widened, and her jaw went slack. *Seriously? The damn creature is answering what I am thinking?* She felt kind of silly as she made a V with two fingers. "Peace…" Her voice came out like a squeaky little mouse.

The dragon said nothing but suddenly began to shrink and change. Her heart skipped a beat, and her skin sizzled with awareness. The same man that had haunted her dreams for years stood before her. He was tall and muscular and built much larger than the men on Pazona. Dark blue hair with reddish and purple tints—the same colors as the dragon's scales—framed his handsome face and enhanced the glowing amber of his eyes.

When she was young, he was a boy, her playmate, romping through forests and climbing trees to her delight, but as she matured, so did he, and he became her dream lover, filling her sleep with passion and desire. They had grown up together in her dreams. During her waking moments, she often fantasized about him and loved having the dreams when she closed her eyes at night. Except, this time, he was a shapeshifting dragon, and that was new and just too damn crazy for words.

See, it is all a stupid dream.

She suppressed a giggle and decided to go along with the dream to see where it would take her next. She looked behind her. The clock face, reflected within the big oval lights, shimmered. It showed three minutes past midnight. If she stepped back into the chest, the dragon would disappear, and she would wake up in her bed.

She was about to turn around when the man grasped her wrist and yanked her away. She almost fell against him. The lights faded, the clock face disappeared, and all that was left was the shiny gold chest on the ground with the normal size clock in it. It did not matter anyway. She would return to the shop as soon as she awoke. Right?

"Where am I? What is this place?" She glanced around. Wherever she was, it was nighttime. Two huge mauve moons lit up the scenery around her. She took in the lush purple grass, the myriad of flowers in different colors and hues, and the tall trees covered in wispy lavender leaves. The place was incredibly beautiful and not one she recognized from her dreams.

He turned her to face him, the fire in his amber eyes holding her entranced. "You have finally returned home."

Azilia swallowed hard, enjoying the feel of him holding her arms a little too much to handle. Her reaction to him in life was much more acute than in her dreams. "So the dragon said."

His mouth curved into a sexy smile, making her heart skip a beat.

"The dragon is me."

"There are no dragons in the place I call home, which obviously is not here, so you are a just figment of my imagination just like this place." Taking a step back, she freed herself from his grip, then peered up at him. This was so much different from her nightly escapades. So much more real...so much more intense. "Who the hell are you anyway? I have seen you in my dreams often, but you have never told me your name."

"I am Jasim, your chosen consort at birth." He bowed his head slightly to her, then took her hand in is and kissed her fingers sending shivers down her spine. "And you are Princess Islea."

"You are my consort? And I am a princess?" She shook her head and muttered under her breath. "This illusion is getting better and better."

"I know this may be hard for you to believe, but this is no dream, and I am not an illusion. You are on the planet Zuynus. Your parents are King Nuret and Queen Mirra."

All of this was crazy. One moment she was Chief Engineer aboard The Cepheus, and the next her whole world had been turned inside out. Her grandmother had said she appeared in the chest the night her mother had given birth to a dead infant. She was so different from the rest of her family. An anomaly. Her whole life had been a lie. If any of this was even real.

"I have never heard of such a planet, and I have traveled to many. What makes you think I am this Princess Islea?"

"Twenty-six years ago, the infant princess disappeared along with the chest and the clock inside it." He brushed his fingers through her hair. "You could be your mother's twin. I do not doubt that you are the princess."

"My grandmother found the chest inside a cave on Pazona, my home planet. How did I end up inside that chest twenty-six years ago? And where did the dead baby she had put in it disappear to?"

"Twenty-six years ago, our scientists created the portal, which was the chest in combination with two clocks. The portal would allow travel to galaxies beyond our own, something that our space technology had not been able to achieve. The information had somehow been leaked to the planet Lanurque. They had been our enemy for many years. Learning of the portal, they coveted the secret to creating their own, and on the day Queen Mirra had given birth to you, they invaded.

"The goddess Jantella, who is a powerful sorceress and healer, was in the palace to bless you when the enemy attacked. The queen bundled you within Jantella's medicinal basket and entrusted her infant to the goddess to take you to safety.

"Jantella took you to the science building,

thinking you would be safe there. When she saw a detachment of Lanurque's soldiers approach the building, she placed you within the chest to keep you from harm and stood ready to face the attackers. Her fury was great, and she unleashed her powers on the invaders. Unfortunately, she was too late to stop a barrage of their weapons. During the attack, one of the clocks was damaged, activating the portal. You, the chest, and the other clock inside the chest disappeared almost instantly."

Azilia crossed her arms over her chest and gave him a hard look. "What you are telling me, does not ring true. When my grandmother found the chest, all it had in it was the clock, and it was broken. No baby. Should I not have been in the chest when she found it in the cave?"

"We do not know how the portal worked. It had not yet been tested using a living thing, much less a person. The three scientists that developed the portal fled in fear and were killed when the enemy approached. Much of their equipment and research was destroyed when they managed to fire their weapons before Jantella took care of them. The activation clock was found in bits and pieces among the mess. I suspect this clock was broken when the chest fell on the stone floor of the cave. Our other scientists have been working for years to solve the mystery surrounding the portal and the clocks."

"That still does not answer my question why I was not in the chest when my grandmother found it. And what about the dead infant? Why did she disappear? And how is it that you happened to be at this exact spot at the right time?"

"Jantella told me I had to be in this location at this exact time. She did not tell me why, nor do I have the answers to your questions, and I know nothing of a dead infant. Perhaps Jantella can explain what happened to both of us, and how it is that we invaded each other's dreams." Jasim reached out and gently squeezed her fingers, then stepped back. "Come with me to the palace. Your parents will be overjoyed to know you are alive and well."

Azilia studied him a moment. His amber eyes reflected the same confusion she felt. She inclined her head in assent, then looked around for transport of some kind but saw none. When he suddenly began to change into a dragon right before her eyes, she stepped back and held her breath. The majestic beast reappeared. He began to rise, picked her up with one claw, and with the other, he grabbed the chest.

This is not *happening! Time to wake up now. Stop this dream. Dream*? It was becoming a nightmare. She was on an alien planet held by a dragon's claw, and they were flying at high speed.

"Put me down!" she yelled, to no avail.

The flight seemed to take forever as she shivered against the chill in the air. Jasim finally descended toward the courtyard of a large palace. Before he touched the ground, he carefully set her and the chest on the stone pavers. In seconds, the dragon disappeared, and again the man stood in its place.

Azilia's gaze locked with his. In the soft lights of the tall lamps that illuminated the courtyard, she could see him much better, and damn did he set her blood on fire. She had never felt attracted to a male before...except for him...in her dreams. But he was a fantasy man, conjured up by her subconscious. *Wasn't he?* Her body did not think so. She felt the chemistry between them growing stronger every moment they were together.

Her pheromones were raging out of control. *Get a grip on yourself, girl.* His amber eyes glittered with amusement, annoying her.

She turned her attention to the palace. "This place is enormous. Where to now?"

"To the royal quarters. We will wake your parents."

"You are joking. It is the middle of the night."

"And they will not mind if we wake them. Not for this."

The guards automatically stepped aside as they approached the large, beautifully carved wooden doors. Jasim opened them and waved her inside. Hesitantly, she stepped into a huge foyer that reeked of wealth. Beautiful marble statues stood everywhere. Large marble pots held blooming plants. Tall vases that had some kind of tall silvery ferns in them stood scattered here and there. The floor was so shiny it almost appeared to be made of glass. Chandeliers draped from the ceiling. At the far end, a wide, circular staircase covered with rich red carpet, led to the next level.

"Up the stairs," Jasim told her while hooking her arm through his.

She shivered, but not from cold this time. His touch sent tingles all the way up her arm, to her stomach, down her back. *Oh well, the dream can continue for a while.* Maybe he would end up kissing her…or more. That caused her to giggle.

"What is funny?"

"This dream."

"Islea, it is not a dream. I have told you this several times. Though I *would* truly like to kiss and taste you."

Oh my God! I have to watch what I think.

"My name is Azilia."

"Not here it is not."

He halted in front of double gilded doors. They had a small crown embedded in the center of each, and a guard stood on either side. Jasim nodded at one of the guards. "We need to see His Majesty. It is urgent."

Now, in the brilliant light of the hallway, she noticed the markings on Jasim's forehead, the sides of his face, and his neck. He had the same scaly skin condition as her, though she did not recall his scales in her dreams.

Coincidence? It is a dream, stupid. Anything is possible in a dream.

Jasim traced his fingers along her temple, then dropped his hand. "Not a dream, canterra. We are the same species."

Her breath hitched. The name was familiar, one he had called her many times in her fantasies. "How can this possibly be real?"

Before he could answer, a man dressed in a long red robe opened the door. "Jasim, what is it? Why—"

"Your Majesty, this is—"

The king did not allow him to finish. He pushed the door wider, and taking Azilia by the arm, yanked her inside. He clapped twice, and a brilliant light lit the large room. Grabbing both her arms, he held her at arm's length and studied her face.

"It cannot be. Is it? She is Mirra's double. Almost. After all this time? Is it possible?"

"Nuret, what is going on? What is all the commotion about? Who is —" The woman who had just joined the king gazed at Azilia with wide eyes, then fell in a crumpled heap of voluminous nightgown and robe on the floor.

The king rushed to his wife. "Mirra, dear...wake up. It is Islea. Just like Jantella predicted it would be, the impossible has happened. Wake up, Mirra!"

The queen's eyes opened, and she gazed at Azilia for what seemed like a very long time. Azilia in return scrutinized her. They looked so much alike, the woman on the floor could indeed be her twin, though somewhat older.

"How is this possible?" The queen took the king's hand and stood, then ran to Azilia and embraced her.

They were the same height, had the same color hair, and the facial resemblance was overwhelming. Azilia stood in the woman's embrace awkwardly, but she suffered it. If she was indeed this woman's lost baby, she imagined how Mirra must have suffered so many years ago.

The queen sobbed and would not let go of Azilia until the king gently disengaged the queen's clutching hands, wrapped an arm around her, and led her to a chair.

"This calls for a strong drink." He fetched a full flask and four glasses, then filled the glasses and handed one to each.

"Jasim, you have much explaining to do," the king said while taking his wife's shaking hand in his.

Jasim took a drink from his glass, then set it on the table. "Jantella came to see me yesterday and told me it was of the utmost importance that I fly to the location where the old science building used to be. I had to be there at midnight exactly and wait. She would not explain why. I was dubious, but one does not argue with the goddess, so I went. At just after midnight, the golden chest appeared, along with the portal, and this young woman stepped through it."

"Unbelievable." The king shook his head. "I feel as if this is a dream."

"I am in complete agreement with you there, Your Majesty. This is a dream. It has to be," Azilia said. She looked at Jasim. "I gather your people won the war?"

"Yes. The enemy could not withstand an army of dragons. After Jantella took you to safety, the king contacted the dragon council. Within the hour, our army gathered, and the enemy was defeated," Jasim told her.

"Are all the people on this planet dragons?" Azilia asked.

Jasim chuckled. "No. We were the first to live on Zuynus. Many years later, people who escaped from a dying planet arrived and settled here. We have lived in peace with them for many centuries."

"Islea, where have you been all these years?" the queen asked in a trembling voice.

"My planet is called Pazona, and if you do not mind stepping out of my dream, all three of you, I would like to wake up now." She took a hard swallow of her drink causing her to cough and sputter. It was strong, much stronger than she had ever had.

"Your clothes—"

Her hand flew to her chest, touching the material of her jumpsuit. It was the only thing that was normal about this whole situation. "This is my uniform. I am Chief Engineer aboard the spaceship The Cepheus."

"Our daughter? An engineer? On a spaceship?" The king scrunched his forehead.

"Look, the crazy lights that came out of that chest are what is causing this nightmare." Azilia turned to Jasim, her heart beating a mile a minute. She normally was not one to panic, but this illusion needed to end. "I need the chest so that I can stop it somehow."

"I left the chest in the courtyard. I will have a guard bring it in." He gently squeezed her arm, then got up to go to the doors.

She heard him talking to the guards outside, then turned her attention back to the king and queen. "I am sorry. I am not your daughter. My parents live on Pazona. Well, my mother does. My father died a while back. And I need to go home because tomorrow is Christmas Eve. Everyone will wonder where I am."

"My dear, I have never heard of the planet Pazona," the king said.

"And I have never heard of Zuynus. There is no such planet, and because my ship has jump capability, I have traveled to many galaxies throughout the universe."

Jasim returned and sat next to her. "I have already explained this is a different galaxy she has not yet visited, but she does not believe me. She needs to speak with Jantella." He turned to Azilia. "You talked of lights coming from the chest. Can you explain to us what you were doing when the lights began?"

She brushed her fingers through her hair, then rubbed her face. The whole situation was tiring. She just wanted to return home and crawl into bed. Maybe when she woke up the nightmare would be over. "I had finished cleaning and fixing the clock, set the correct time, and put it back inside the chest. When I went to close the lid is when the lights appeared, and a strong force pulled me into the chest."

Jasim shifted in his chair and crossed his legs. "Ah, that explains something at least. By fixing the clock, you must have activated the mechanism for the portal. Somehow, the portal took you back to the exact location from which you departed."

"That still does not explain why my grandmother did not find me in the chest until the next morning. Nor how the dead baby disappeared."

The king studied her a moment, his face still filled with amazement. "Please, tell us everything? Maybe hearing your story will help to decipher what happened."

Azilia told him about the premature birth of the baby and her grandmother placing the dead infant inside the chest. "No one ever knew that I was not my parents' real child. My strange appearance was contributed to an anomaly caused by premature birthing."

"But my dear, you look so much like me at that age. Surely you see the striking resemblance between us?" The queen's eyes glistened with tears threatening to spill again.

Azilia felt bad for the royals, but she sure as

hell could not stay in this place. She had a life, a family…a job. Even if she were stuck in the antique shop for two years, she would eventually return to her ship. Her grandmother had opened a can of worms with her letter, and right now she wanted no part of it. "If I activated the portal by fixing the clock, I should be able to do it again and go home."

The queen jumped up. "No. You will not leave me again, daughter. Now that you are finally found and back with us, I will not let you out of my sight. We are your real parents, your true family."

"You had no other children?" Azilia dared to ask.

"No. Something happened when I gave birth to you causing me to become barren. You are the crown princess. One day you will rule Zuynus with Jasim by your side," the queen said patiently.

Azilia heaved a huge sigh that seemed to come from the depth of her soul. None of this was on her agenda. *Queen? Rule a whole planet?* Not if she could help it. *I'm sorry, Groma, but I cannot be this person. I am Azilia. Not some lost princess.*

"You do realize you are a dragon, like us?" Jasim asked softly.

"Oh, this is priceless. You will be telling me

next that I can shapeshift like you."

"Yes, you can."

"How?"

"That is not something I can teach you in a few minutes, but you are capable of it, the same as all of us are. There is an initiation ceremony you must go through before your abilities surface. We all go through the ceremony when we are sixteen."

There was a knock on the door. When Jasim jumped up and opened the door, a guard brought the chest inside and set it on the floor.

Azilia ran to the chest and opened the lid. When she reached for the clock, Jasim stopped her. "No, you will not try to activate the portal. It could be dangerous. You could end up anywhere, even on a deserted star."

Damn! Damn! Damn! This is ridiculous. Wake up Azilia. It is time to get up.

Nothing happened. She was still sitting in a large, beautifully furnished royal room with a king, a queen, and a dragon.

"You need to stop thinking you are in a dream," the dragon man told her. "This is very real, and *we* are real."

"Right. And I can shapeshift into a dragon," she threw back at him.

"Exactly."

"Something else just crossed my mind. How

is it we can understand each other? I do not know your language, and you do not know mine. See, I told you it is all a nightmarish dream because in dreams anything is possible," Azilia said.

Jasim smiled patiently. "We are an ancient race and speak all languages in the universe."

"You have never heard of Pazona. How could you know its language?"

"It comes naturally to us. It is a gift from the gods. Space travelers need universal translators. We do not."

"Must be handy," Azilia muttered. "I would not mind having that ability when I am on missions."

"We are all very tired, and it seems many of our questions still have no answers. Since you have slightly outgrown the nursery we readied for you, Jasim will take you to a guest room where you can rest for the night. I will summon Jantella, and we will continue this in the morning." The king cocked his head at Jasim. "Stay with her. Make sure she does not try to escape."

"No, I want to be with my —" the queen began.

"My dear, this has all been a big shock for us, but also for our daughter. She needs to rest and absorb her new surroundings and life."

"I will not let her out of my sight," Jasim told the king.

Jasim went to take her arm, but Azilia shook his hand off. "I can walk on my own, thank you."

He led her to a room not far from the royal chambers, just as ornate, and gorgeous.

Azilia fell on the bed and though she fought against it, felt her eyelids droop. Until now, she had not realized how tired she was. If she gave in to sleep, she would wake up in the morning in her bedroom above the antique shop, and life would be back to normal, so she allowed herself to drift off.

CHAPTER FOUR

Someone coming into Azilia's room woke her up. It had to be her mother being the only other person to have a key to Antique Trove. "Mother? What are you doing here?" she said sleepily and yawned.

"It is time to get up for breakfast," a man said. "We are joining the king and queen in their quarters."

What? A man? She looked in the direction of the voice and saw him stretched out in a large chair, his feet on a stool.

It was no dream. She was still in the palace. And the dragon man was real.

"A servant brought clean clothing for you. Bathing facilities are over there." He pointed to a door.

Sending him a glare, she jumped out of bed, then suddenly realized she was naked. Yanking a sheet off the bed, she wrapped it around herself. "You...you...did not... I am ready to clout—"

"Not to worry. I had one of the servants come in to take your clothes off. I could not let you sleep in that dirty suit."

"How come I never woke up when she undressed me? What was in that drink I had?"

"Nothing, but it is very potent. Especially if you are not used to such strong spirits."

"And where were you when the servant undressed me?" she demanded.

"Right here. I closed my eyes."

"Uh huh! You are a man! Like I believe you."

He grinned. "Believe what you like."

His smile was disarming. Azilia found it difficult to stay mad at him. Clutching the sheet around her body, she went to the door he had pointed out. She gasped as she viewed the luxurious bathroom and the sunken tub that bubbled invitingly.

"Would you like me to wash your back?" he asked innocently and grinned again.

"No, I can wash my own back. Thanks." But

oh damn, just the thought of his hands on her back set her blood coursing through her veins. "It is Christmas Eve, and I have to get home," she muttered to herself.

The bubbling hot perfumed water relaxed her. She could have stayed in it a lot longer, but she needed to get to the chest and see if she could activate that damn portal. She hoped it was still in the royal chambers.

Draped in a towel, she came out of the bathroom and looked at the clothing hanging over the back of a chair. "I want my suit. I am not wearing a fluffy dress!"

"Then you will go to breakfast wearing a towel. Your suit is getting cleaned. You have no choice, Islea."

"Stop calling me that." She lifted the dress off the chair and admired it. It was beautiful. Grecian style in a pale mauve color. The material was a shiny satin studded with tiny jewels embroidered on it in intricate floral patterns. She pulled it over her head and dropped the towel in the process.

Blood raced to her face as she stood naked from her neck down. Quickly she pulled the dress down and over her hips. Last, she draped a gorgeous lace shawl around her shoulders.

"You are very beautiful, Islea. I am proud to be your consort."

"I was gone. Supposedly dead all these years. Why did you not marry someone else?" She swiveled and saw his hungry gaze on her. It caused a strange throbbing in her belly. By the gods, the man had a weird effect on her.

"Your death was never proven. Therefore, I had to remain your consort until there was proof of your demise. Without a body, that was impossible. I often felt I was destined to remain alone for the rest of my very long life."

"A strange custom."

"I am glad. Because now that we have met I would desire no other woman to share my bed."

"As if I will *ever* share your bed."

Jasim stood, approached her and cupped her cheek. He gazed down at her, heat blazing in his eyes. "You are not the only one who dreams, and you have haunted mine for years, canterra. In my dreams, we join and become one."

Her breath hitched. Had they shared the same dreams? Surely not? "In my dreams, there is no joining." She was going to the hell her father spoke of for lying. "I am ready. And I am starving."

"Ready to share my bed? Starving for me?" he grinned widely and winked. "Let us join the royals." He gallantly opened the door for her. "After you, my beautiful lady."

She noticed that he must have bathed and

changed sometime during the night. He looked even hotter than before, in his leather pants and tunic with polished black boots.

She sighed. If she finally had to fall for a man, did he have to be a dragon? Then again, she was supposedly a dragoness. *Groma, you wanted me to find my roots, where I came from, and I did. I think. I wish I could talk to you.*

Just before they entered the royal quarters, Azilia asked, "Jasim, what kind of work do you do?"

"I am in charge of the king's fleet. My title is, General Jasim Obius Tarangana."

"Fleet? You command a ship? You go on missions?"

"Yes, to all of those questions. You see, canterra, we have a lot in common." *There is that damn smile again.*

As they walked into the royal chambers, Azilia was gratified to see the chest still standing where it had been earlier. The king and queen were already seated at the breakfast table, waiting for them.

"Good morning. Did you sleep well?" the queen asked.

"Like a log."

It was strange looking at the queen now that she was dressed, and her hair was brushed. It was the same color as Azilia's. Looking at the woman was like looking in a mirror. They even wore dresses of the same color and design.

She had no choice but to accept what had happened, and that these were her true parents. Her roots. Never in her wildest dreams could she have conjured up this imaginary tale. It was all real. The chest and clock were a portal, and it had taken her back to where she had come from.

Servants came in with platters of food. Azilia was not really hungry, but she did eat a little bit. Perusing the servants, she noticed they looked different from the royals. They were quite short in stature, stocky, and had no hair. Instead, their skulls were covered with fleshy ridges. Between the ridges were rows of small black dots. Their hands only had four digits, and they had really big feet. *Where did these people originally come from?*

The king finally spoke. "I have asked Jantella to join us after breakfast. Maybe she can shed some light on what occurred twenty-six years ago."

Deep down Azilia knew that what her grandmother had told her in the letter was true, and though she hated to admit it, the king and queen had to be her biological parents.

"I have finally accepted that this is not a dream and have to admit it is real. But please, I have only ever known one father and mother in my life. I do not want to hurt you, but for now, we are strangers to one another." Azilia sighed deeply. "The only thing I ask is that you adopt the name I have been called my whole life, Azilia, and allow me to figure out the portal to return home to my family." When she saw a flash of pain in the queen's eyes, she softly added, "My other family."

"It will be difficult for me to think of you as Azilia when in my thoughts and heart you have been Islea all these years. But we can try. We will speak to Jantella about the portal, but truthfully, it scares me. What if you are lost to us forever?" The fear in the queen's eyes was clear to see.

"If she travels through the portal, I will accompany her. I will not let her go alone," Jasim promised.

"I was the one who fixed the clock, thereby fixing the mechanism to activate the portal. Would the settings not remain the same unless someone else changes them?" Azilia asked.

Breakfast was a five-course meal and seemed to take forever. When it was finally over, and they retired to the living area. The king rang a bell, and a servant appeared bearing a tray laden with a teapot and cups. After placing them on the table, he turned to the king.

"Your Majesty, the goddess Jantella has

arrived."

"Thank you Arnov. Please show her in," the king instructed.

A woman entered. She, too, had small scales on her face and neck. She wore a green flowing gown, edged in silver embroidered flowers and vines that matched her scales. Long silver hair tumbled around her shoulders in thick waves. The woman appeared to be young, yet the wisdom of the ages glowed in her otherworldly golden eyes.

"Jantella, thank you for coming on such short notice." The king approached Jantella, and taking her by the hand, led her to one of the comfortable couches. "Come and sit with us and allow our daughter to tell her tale. Then you can explain to her what happened the night she disappeared. Would you like tea?" the king asked. "Azilia, you can begin telling Jantella what happened so many years ago, how the portal activated, and how you arrived here last night."

Azilia told the goddess everything, then ended with a final question. "What I would like to know is how my grandmother placed a dead baby in the chest with the broken clock, yet she did not find me inside the chest until the morning, and the other infant was gone. It does not make sense." She studied Jantella a moment. The goddess's face held nothing but compassion.

"I knew this day would finally come. I have tried for many years to bring you home, Princess, but to no avail." Jantella placed her teacup on the table and gazed at each one of them. A single tear slid down her cheek.

"On the night of the attack, the enemy seemed to be everywhere. I could not fight them while I was carrying the infant and make it to the safety of the forest. My only option was to hide in the science building, to which there was a clear path at that point. Several Lanurque soldiers had followed me. For Islea's protection against their attack, I placed her within the chest and shielded it with magic. Too late, I realized my powers had opened the portal. When the chest and clock disappeared, I tried everything within me to keep Islea here, and it seemed to work for a few moments. Instead, she had disappeared, and another infant lay on the floor where the chest had stood."

The queen gasped. "Jantella, why did you not tell us this? What happened to the other baby?"

Jantella took the queen's hand. "Forgive me, Mirra. I know how you have suffered these many years, but please, let me finish."

The queen nodded her ascent.

Jantella continued her story. "When the portal closed, I feared it had killed the princess and altered her appearance. I had to defeat the enemy soldiers first. Afterward, when I approached the little one, the baby was so still, almost lifeless. She was so tiny and fragile with skin that was paper thin and tinged blue. The moment I touched her, her body began to glow with a golden light. A deep breath shuddered through her, and she let out a robust wail. I knew then, as I held her in my arms that she was not the princess and that the gods had meant for me to find her."

Azilia pushed herself from the table, her chair falling to the floor. She could hardly believe what she was hearing. "Wait. The baby lived? What did you do with her?"

"My daughter, please sit. We will get to the bottom of this," the king told her, then turned to Jantella. "I am quite troubled that you hid this information from us. I assume since the infant survived the portal that she is alive and well. Where is the young woman now?"

Azilia settled in her seat, then gazed at Jantella. "Please, I must know."

Jantella nodded. "I understand. But first I must explain my actions." She looked at the king and queen. "If you had known of the infant, you would have wanted to raise her as your own. Tissara is an alien. She would never have been permitted to rule as queen. The dragon council would not have allowed it. You know this."

"That would not have mattered to us, Jantella," The queen said in a shaky voice.

Jantella patted the queen's hand. "The gods had other plans for Tissara and your daughter. Without Tissara, I would never have been able to locate Islea." She stood and motioned to the chamber doors. "Now, allow me to introduce, Tissara."

Jantella quickly approached the doors and opened it. Azilia heard her speak softly to the guard. A few moments passed, and then a young woman stepped into the room. Jantella led her to the sitting area. "This is my adoptive daughter, Tissara."

Azilia's hands flew to her face. Tissara looked very much like her mother. She had the same dark hair, bright blue eyes, and the ridges on her forehead were just as pronounced. By her appearance, she looked to be a full-blooded Pazonan.

Azilia approached Tissara, and when she reached out and touched her, their hands began to glow, the light spreading, enveloping them both in its radiance, then suddenly it dissipated in a shower of sparks.

Shock registered through Azilia. "What in the hell just happened?"

Tissara smiled at her. "It is as Mother told me. Once you and I were together, the portal would be complete."

Azilia scrunched up her face and mumbled under her breath, "That really doesn't answer my question."

"Jantella, what is going on?" The king motioned for them to be seated. "Please continue your story."

Azilia sat down by Jasim and Tissara took a chair next to Jantella. She took a deep breath. Her life really had become a real-life nightmare. *And what could it possibly mean that the portal is complete?*

Azilia felt Jasim's hand squeeze her leg. "All will be well, canterra," he whispered close to her ear.

Jantella cleared her throat. "When the clocks the scientists created were damaged, there was no place for that power to go. The portal would have grown exponentially, then exploded, destroying both planets, and if the portal had not been activated, both infants would have died. Tissara as a stillborn and Islea at the hands of our enemies." She gazed at Tissara and then Azilia. "Instead the gods saved them both — and us. The two girls hold the power of the portal within them, and now that they have been united, they have the ability to summon a portal of their own."

"That means I can return home to Pazona, does it not?" Excitement vibrated through Azilia's body. Yes, she wanted to get to know her true family, find out all about her roots, but she had a family on Pazona who loved her, and who she loved just as much. Taking regular trips back and forth would be no different than going out on a mission.

"Yes, you both have the power within you to create a portal," Jantella said.

"And would I be able to return here?"

"Yes. But I would hesitate to test it. You were lost to the king and queen many years ago. To lose you again, would be even more devastating."

"I am willing to risk it. I cannot just abandon the family I have had all my life."

"I would like to accompany you if it is all right?" Tissara asked. "I have longed to meet my real mother all of my life."

"She does not know about you, or that I am not her real daughter. Please allow me to break the news to her first?" Azilia felt nothing but compassion for Tissara, but she could not drop a bomb like this on her mother without some warning. Especially on Christmas Eve.

Tissara nodded, but Azilia could see the disappointment in her eyes. "I understand."

"It will not be for long. A couple of days maybe? That will give me a chance to break the news to my family." Azilia looked at the earnest faces of her birth mother and father. "It is a very important time for my family right now. It is essential that I be present for my...adoptive family."

The king took the queen's hand in his. "You may try, and we will pray to the gods that you arrive safely at the designated destination and return to us again."

"I will not leave her side," Jasim said.

"How do I activate the portal? Do I use the clock like I did last night?"

"Visualize the place you wish to be, then draw a circle in front of you with your finger. That will open the portal for you," Jantella informed her.

"Sounds easy enough."

Jantella stood and held her hand out to Tissara. "We will now leave you in peace."

Tissara shook her head. "I would like to stay here if that is all right. Azilia may need my assistance with the portal."

"Yes, please. I do not need anything to go wrong," Azilia said.

The king nodded his ascent. "Tissara is

welcome to stay."

Jantella sighed, and with one last look at her adoptive daughter, left the royal chambers.

"Then we will wait until midnight," Jasim told her. "Meanwhile, I am sure your father and mother want to spend time with you, get to know you. You can tell them all about your childhood, your schooling, your growing years, and your family on that other world."

She could easily fall in love with this man. Besides him being hotter than anyone she had ever met — sometimes obnoxious and bossy — he had a wise streak. He had humor and was a real gentleman. Yes, he was allowed to be her king.

Azilia spent the whole day and evening with her true parents, Tissara, and Jasim. She learned so much about them, the planet, about him, and in turn, they heard her life story.

"This Christmas, it is important?" the king asked.

"My adoptive father was from Earth. Christmas is a traditional family holiday on that planet. We all give each other gifts and have a big dinner. It is the one day of the year where the whole family gets together. I have twelve brothers and sisters on Pazona, all married with children."

"That is a very big family." Tissara's gaze

held a look of wonder. "That means I have that many brothers and sisters, too. Thirteen. I feel as if you are my sister."

Azilia never mentioned the two years she had committed to. Or did that matter anymore? Her grandmother had hoped she would find her roots. She had found them, and quite fast. And did she want to give up her career as Chief Engineer? No, not at this point.

The king had canceled all his commitments for that morning and afternoon. They had lunch together and spent the whole afternoon talking. Then after dinner, they continued sharing stories long into the night.

"I should return to Pazona now. I have already missed Christmas Eve dinner. I am sure my mother is worried sick because I am not answering her calls." Azilia dabbed her mouth with her napkin, then set it on the table. "Do you think it best if we return to the spot I entered your world?"

"It is not necessary. The magic is within us. Mother had me practice even though I would not be able to open a portal until we met and activated that power. I will show you what she taught me," Tissara offered.

"Thank you." Azilia rubbed her chin. "I would rather be safe and go to the spot where I arrived. We should bring the chest and clock, too, just in case," she told Jasim.

"We want to go with you to see you off," the queen told her.

"Are you sure?"

"Yes. Come. We will leave from the courtyard."

"You can ride on my neck instead of me picking you up," Jasim told her. "All you need to do is climb onto my leg and then to my neck."

"It would help if I could turn into the dragon you said I could."

He smiled and melted her heart. "All in good time."

She waited until the three of them changed to their dragons, then climbed onto Jasim's leg and then to his neck while Tissara climbed onto the queen's.

"Hold on to my scales tight."

Jasim carried the chest in one of his claws. The journey seemed shorter than her initial flight to the palace. Before she could wonder, they arrived at the same spot where she had come through the portal. How he knew the exact location, she had no idea. He set the chest down first before he landed and waited for her to climb down before he shifted.

Azilia had no idea if the portal was going to work. The queen and king both hugged her and extracted another promise from her that she would return.

"Take care of our girl, Jasim," the king told him.

Azilia lifted the lid of the chest and took the clock out. It showed the exact time when the portal had first appeared at Antique Trove. She went to close the lid, but nothing happened this time.

Tissara stood in front of her. "Mother said we would not need the chest and clock anymore. Remember her words? Do as she instructed, visualize the location, then draw a circle in the air with your fingers."

Azilia did as she was told and almost instantly a burst of light flashed from her fingertips to form an oval, increasing in size and brightness. She tightened the grip on Jasim's hand as she felt the light pulling her into it. The same spinning sensation, dizziness, and blinding headache that assaulted her before forced her to close her eyes. Then when she opened them again, she was back inside Antique Trove.

"Jasim?" she whispered.

"Yes, I am here."

She turned to see him standing behind her. "We are in the shop my grandmother left to me after she died. Now that we are on my territory, there is more I need to tell you."

"Should I be afraid?"

She chuckled. "I will tell you everything later. For now, I need to get some sleep. Tomorrow is going to be a hellishly busy day. I have not even wrapped gifts. That will be first on the list in the morning. Come with me, I will show you to your room."

"Everything is very different here."

"Yes, of course. You are on another planet. And tomorrow morning it will be Christmas Day, and I will wake up to find this has all been one bizarre dream." Azilia grinned.

The other guest room was opposite hers. She opened the door for him, then turned and opened the door to her room. "Goodnight, Jasim. It has been the adventure of a lifetime."

He acted so fast that Azilia hardly had time to react. One second she was ready to close her door, the next she was in his arms, and his lips were on hers.

She had never been kissed by a man.

No man had ever shown interest in her, not those from Pazona, or any of the alien men she had met on her missions. Men from Earth looked the most like her, but none of them had ever seemed to be attracted to her. Of course not. Her stupid skin scared them off.

The chemistry with Jasim shouted out within her...aching to be released. Her pheromones had gone berserk…again.

Her lips parted under his. He kissed her tenderly at first, then his arms tightened around her, and her simmering blood went into a full boil as he sucked her tongue into his mouth. His hands cupped her buttocks and kneaded gently.

Since this is one wild dream, I might as well enjoy this hotter than hell man…

The kiss lasted a long time, and she never wanted it to end. He walked her backward into her room until they got to her bed.

Suddenly, he tore his lips away from hers and gazed into her eyes. "I have fallen in love with you, my precious princess."

Love? Was this truly love that she was feeling? This wild attraction? This crazy longing to have him kiss her again, to crawl into his arms and stay there forever?

"Yes, I feel it too, Jasim," she answered softly.

"We have to wait until we are officially joined. Goodnight, my dragon princess."

He left her feeling suddenly empty and alone, and reluctantly she peeled off her dress and climbed into bed.

Sleep did not come easy. Azilia's hormones were raging, and she had to use all her willpower not to go to Jasim's room and crawl into bed with him.

CHAPTER FIVE

The pinging from the tablet was a rude awakening. Azilia struggled to open her eyes and hit the receive button. Lying on her side, she gazed at her mother in the holograph that appeared. "Yes, Mother?"

"Where were you yesterday? You did not come for Christmas Eve dinner. Neither did you answer my calls. I was worried about you. Merry Christmas, honey. What time are you coming, Zilly? I could use your help."

"Sorry about yesterday, Mother. I was busy sorting things in the shop, and I did not have my tablet with me. Time just slipped away.

Right now, I am not even dressed yet. You woke me."

"Girl, breakfast is almost ready. Hurry up."

"I have not packed my gifts yet."

"Are you sick?" her mother asked worriedly.

"No, Mother, I told you, I have been very busy with the shop. Let me go so I can get up and get ready."

"See you soon. Wear something pretty for a change instead of your uniform."

She hit the end call button and swung her legs over the side of the bed. After yawning and stretching, she jumped up resolutely, opened the door to go to the bathroom, only to run into the man from her dream.

Oh, my God! It was not a dream.

"Jasim…I…"

When his gaze raked her from head to toe and back again, she suddenly realized she was naked. But so was he. *Damn!* In a glance, she saw the small scales on his arms, on his abdomen, taken in his toned body with cords of muscle that shaped his entire form from wide shoulders to trim waist, his bold thighs, and calves.

Blood rushed to her head, heating her face. She quickly jumped back into her room and slammed the door. Grabbing her robe, she put it on, then opened the door again, to find him still standing there…naked.

She gathered her wits and stood straight. "I am going to the bathroom to shower. After that, I have to wrap gifts and then we are going to my parents' home. We will have breakfast there. I have not gone shopping yet, so there is very little food in the house. I can make you some coffee…"

"Coffee?"

"Yes. We are wasting time. It is late, and my mother is waiting." She hurried to the kitchen, plugged in the coffee pot, then rushed to the bathroom.

Trying to wrap her mind around her dream that was not a dream, she showered and went to the kitchen for a much-needed coffee.

"I finally figured out how to use your bathroom." Jasim joined her in the kitchen.

Azilia felt the blood rush to her face again. He only wore pants. The desire to run her hands over those sculpted pecs was great. Trying to squash the feeling, she sipped from her coffee, then filled a mug for him.

"What did you call this?"

"Coffee. It is a beverage that people on Earth drink. It is grown on Pazona now, and our people have taken quite a liking to it. My father could not do without his morning coffee."

"This shop, you mentioned it was your

grandmother's."

"Yes. I inherited it. Her last letter to me states she wants me to live here for two years and operate the shop, but that was because she wanted me to find my roots. I have found my roots now, so I can go back to my regular work and hire someone to take care of the shop."

"Do not forget you are a royal princess. In the future, your job will be to rule as queen of Zuynus."

"Yes, well...I cannot think about that right now. I need to get dressed and wrap gifts." It was not the right time to tell him that she planned to resume her career as Chief Engineer.

"I do not have a change of clothing with me."

"Mother might still have my father's clothes. Or better yet, I can quickly wash these for you. I will give you a robe." She fetched a robe from her room and handed it to him. He put it on, and she burst out laughing. The robe looked like it would burst at the seams and barely covered his lower region.

Azilia was glad her grandmother had recently invested in the most modern washer slash dryer appliance. It cleaned and dried clothing and linens in fifteen minutes. She threw his clothes into the machine, then hurried down the stairs to begin wrapping gifts.

He had followed her. "Can I help?"

"Sure. Just watch what I do. I am taking the easy way out. Boxes with a bow on top."

The pile grew and grew. Azilia knew she would need to call her mother to come and get them. It would never all fit in a minicab. Or…she could call a maxicab. Yes, she would do that. Her mother was probably flustered enough already and her coming out of the shop with a man, would only cause raised eyebrows and too many questions.

When Jasim's clothes were done, she handed them to him. "We need to hurry. It is nearly lunchtime, and we have not eaten anything yet."

Azilia looked in her wardrobe. She always wore her uniform, even to family gatherings. Her gaze fell on the dress at the foot of the bed, the one from Zuynus. She could wear it. Her mother would be surprised. And the shawl…it would make a fantastic gift for her mother.

The maxicab she had called arrived, and they carried the full bags of gifts to it.

"It would be easier for my dragon to transport the bags and us, and probably faster," Jasim grumbled when he hoisted the last bag into the cab.

"Right. And freak out my whole family. Not to mention the population here."

In the cab, on the way to her parents' house,

she thought about how to explain Jasim to her family. Where had she met him? There was no way she could tell her mother, or the family, where she was really from, who she was. Not today. The knowledge that she was no kin, would devastate her mother and she refused to ruin her family's Christmas. She would have to speak to her mother alone another time.

"You have to tell her the truth, Azilia," Jasim said. "Your mother has raised you since birth, but she deserves to know all of it. She has the right to know of Tissara."

"I will. Just not today." She hated that he could read her thoughts. "I wish you would stay out of my mind. My thoughts are my own. You listening to them is an invasion of my privacy."

"I am sorry. We can turn communication on and off. You will learn all this, too."

"I am not sure I want the ability to read people's minds," she grumbled. "I was wondering how to introduce you. How did we meet? Where are you from? No one has ever heard of Zuynus. We need to think about this before we go inside and meet my mother. And some of the family is probably already there, too."

"Mm, I see the problem. How about Zuynus is a very small planet at the edge of the universe? You met me when you were sent there on a mission. Does that make sense?"

"Right. Watch some of my older nephews and nieces start investigating this small planet and find out there is no such place."

"Maybe it is so small that it was never documented?"

"Then why would they send my ship there on a mission?"

Jasim frowned. "I know what you can say. Your ship experienced technical difficulties. You found the planet and landed on Zuynus to effect repairs and met me during your time there."

Azilia thought about that for a moment. "That is one explanation. How do we explain that you have the same markings on your skin as me? Your weird color hair? And how and when did you get here?"

"I am...what did you call it? An anomaly? Like you? And I am here with my ship to visit your planet?"

"What a fucking predicament this is. Maybe you should not go with me. You can stay in the shop."

"I promised your true parents I would not let you out of my sight. Not a chance."

They pulled into the driveway of her parents' estate.

"What is that strange statue? The man

dressed in strange red clothing, sitting in a foreign-looking vehicle, pulled by alien creatures?"

Azilia laughed. "Santa Claus in his sleigh, and the reindeer. I am going to have to teach you a lot."

"It looks very…interesting."

She supposed it would all look very strange to an alien who had never heard of Christmas in his life.

"Do all the people on your planet celebrate this Christmas?" he asked.

"No, not everyone. There are quite a few people from Earth that live here, and many of them continued to celebrate their traditional holiday."

Several of her nephews rushed out to meet them and helped to unload the cab. Azilia smiled at their enthusiasm, and at Jasim's wonderment written all over his face. Her stomach growled. All she wanted was to get inside and eat something as soon as possible.

Her mother was busy in the kitchen just getting ready to put the nigoro birds in the ovens. She always baked three of them to feed their large family. The nigoro bird was the closest to what her father had called a *turkey*. Her mother had learned to adapt to Earth's customs and traditions and had even taught herself many of Earth's recipes. She lived to please her husband.

"Zilly, I am so glad you are here." Her mother hugged her. "And you brought a guest?"

"Yes, I did. Mother, this is Jasim."

Jasim shook her mother's hand. The expression on her mother's face did not escape Azilia.

"Jasim, go and meet everyone else and make yourself at home while I set my daughter to work here," she said.

"Mother, I am starving. We did not have breakfast."

"I told you breakfast was almost ready when I called you. There is plenty to eat in the dining room. Go grab something and then come back to help me."

Azilia led Jasim to the dining room, handed him a plate, and left him to help himself. Grabbing a few sandwiches, she hurried back to the kitchen.

"Daughter, you have some explaining to do."

"Today?"

"Yes, today. Who is he? When and how did you meet him? He looks just like you, how is that possible? Tell me, girl."

"Jasim is going to be my husband." Azilia couldn't believe she just blurted that out. *Way to keep your mother from freaking out.*

Her mother almost dropped the bowl she had in her hands. "I have just met him for the first time, and you are already announcing your betrothal?"

Inwardly, Azilia giggled. How would her mother react if she knew that her daughter had only known Jasim for two days? "Yes, Mother."

"How do you know he is the right one? You need to have a lengthy courtship, Zilly. It is too sudden."

"He is the right one, Mother. Stop fussing. You can begin planning our wedding. Is this not what you have wanted for quite a while now? Just the other day you told me it was time to settle down."

Her mother beat the batter in the bowl almost to death. "I find it curious that you would meet a man who has the same skin affliction, the same strangely colored hair. Something does not feel right. Something is not the way it should be."

"I think your batter is more than done, Mother. Stop overreacting. Just be happy that your only single child is stepping into matrimony. Only the other day you were giving me a hard time about settling down and starting a family."

She wondered how Jasim was doing and

what he was saying, and she wished she had his telepathic ability now. It would sure come in handy.

She spent the next few hours in the kitchen with her mother until several of her sisters arrived and pitched in. So far, her mother had kept the big news to herself, but Azilia knew it would not be long before they all knew.

Jasim sat near the Christmas tree gazing at the growing pile of gifts. She joined him. "Have you been bombarded with questions yet?"

"A little. We have to stay until after dinner?"

"Until midnight or beyond. It takes all evening for everyone to unwrap their gifts."

"Oh."

Azilia knew he had to feel as uncomfortable as she had felt in the palace, and in the presence of royalty. "I told Mother that we are betrothed."

His eyebrows shot up. "And? How did she react?"

"Not too well. She is very suspicious and said *something does not feel right. Something is not the way it should be.*"

"Does your mother have special abilities?"

"Not really. She is very intuitive. Her gut feelings are always true. But she has no magic or foresight or anything. Not everyone on our planet is gifted with special powers. Just a few lucky ones are."

"Is the dining room large enough to seat so many?" he wondered.

She giggled. "No, there is no table large enough to seat all of us. We eat smorgasbord style. That means the food is all set up on a large table. When it is ready, we take a plate and utensils, dish up our food, then find a place to sit and eat it. Can be anywhere in the house, even outside. After everyone has eaten and the dishes cleared away, we sing Christmas carols first before we begin opening gifts."

Azilia was glad when dinner was over, the food and dishes cleared away, and her mother sat at the piano. It was another item her father had brought with him from Earth, and her mother had learned to play it to please him. She suddenly stood up from the piano bench and called out to them all.

"Quiet, everyone. We will begin to sing shortly, but first I have an announcement."

Oh, oh. Here it comes. And Azilia was right.

"Azilia and Jasim are betrothed. There is no set date yet, but Azilia has asked me to begin planning the wedding."

The announcement caused quite a stir. Azilia's oldest brother, Quentino, said, "Congratulations. Jasim, tell us, where are you from? How did you meet?"

And so it began. The story...the lies. Azilia hated it, but she had no choice. She told them what they had come up with in the cab. It sounded plausible.

"I find it strange you have the same appearance and markings as our sister. I am not buying any of what you are both telling me," Quentino said.

Her brother was a gifted counselor. He was picking up on their lies. *Oh man, give it up, please.*

Her mother thankfully put a stop to it, but Azilia knew this was not the end of the questioning.

After the Christmas carols, everyone was too busy opening their gifts to think about Jasim and Azilia's betrothal. When it was just past midnight, Azilia decided they should leave.

"You are not staying the night?" her mother questioned. "You will never get a cab now. Unless you booked one?"

"No, I forgot."

Everyone always stayed the night. The mansion had many guest rooms, plenty of beds for everyone. If they ran out of beds because there were more guests than rooms, they camped on couches and chairs. They all had breakfast together the next morning. Azilia did not want to face more questioning, and she knew it would happen. "I will try and call one anyway. Thank you, Mother. Dinner was, as always, delicious."

"Yes, thank you. Eh, what do I call you?" Jasim asked.

"For now, you may call me Stabila. After you are married, you will call me mother."

Her mother hugged her and whispered, "Call me tomorrow?"

Azilia nodded, then pulled back and pretended to order a mini or maxicab. "We will go and wait outside."

"You did not call a cab. How are we going back to your shop?" Jasim asked as he followed her out of the door.

"You are flying us. It is dark. Everyone is busy. No one will see. Come to the road. It is far enough away from the house."

Azilia took the lead and marched to the road. She was disturbed, more than she wanted to be. Christmas was always such a special time. Instead, it had turned into the most awkward day and evening she had ever experienced in her life.

"Okay, you can shift now," she told him.

Jasim changed into his dragon. She was about to get on his leg and climb up to his neck when one of her nephews who must have followed them out, shouted, "Grandmother, Father, Mother, everyone, come and see! There is a dragon outside."

The floodlights flicked on, lighting up the whole property and part of the road. And of course, Jasim's dragon. "Oh, my God! Go! Fly! Just pick me up!"

Several piercing screams came from the verandah. Her mother's loud yell, "Do something, someone, anyone! It is flying away and abducting Azilia. Look, she is hanging in its claws."

Azilia's heart sank to her smallest toe. She heard her mother's words and feared the worst. Her family would contact the authorities. "Fly higher!" she shouted. The wind whipped around her. She shivered. Winter was showing its frosty nose. It would not be long before they saw snow.

Her fear was fully realized when she saw police patrolling below them. Their small crafts sped back and forth between her parents' home and her grandmother's shop located on the outskirts of the city. She hoped Jasim was smart enough to land in a forest somewhere. Surely, he could see the small crafts way below them with their flashing orange lights?

The wind around her became fierce as she felt him speed up more and rise to a higher altitude. It seemed to take forever before he began to descend and landed somewhere far away from home, beyond the dark forest that bordered the city and near the mountains. He set her down gently, then morphed into Jasim, the man.

Snowflakes settled on her face and nose. She shivered, cold to the bone. Jasim stepped toward her and gathered her in his arms. "Come here, my little canterra," he said softly. "Let me warm you."

Heat flowed from him, and she was warm within minutes. What had just happened was still sinking in. "I hope the authorities will blame this whole incident on too much alcohol," she murmured against his chest.

"The boy who saw me shift to my dragon surely did not drink spirits?"

"True. Overactive imagination? But my mother saw you, too, and she does not drink very much. I have no idea how I am going to explain all this."

He held her away and looked deeply into her eyes. "The truth. That is the only option."

Her throat constricted. "Do you realize how it would hurt my mother to know that I am not her true child? I cannot do that to her."

"Your mother is a wise woman. She already knows that all is not as it should be, and she noticed my scales. You can also not go back on your word to her true daughter."

"What does *canterra* mean? You have called

me that several times now."

"It is an endearment in our native language. It is the name of a beautiful, fragile flower."

"Hell, I'm far from fragile," she scoffed and stepped out of his embrace. "We need to figure out a way to get to the shop. There are predators in the forest. We cannot go through it, and it is a long way to the city."

"Ah, my canterra, us dragons have special gifts, powers, also in human form. We can move with incredible speed."

"And once I go through that initiation ceremony you mentioned before, I can do that, too?"

"Yes. For now, I need you to get on my back. Hold on tight."

Azilia jumped up and flung her arms around his neck, then wrapped her legs around his waist.

Jasim lifted his head, sniffed a few times, then began to run. Run? At the speed he was moving he was more like a laser beam. How he could see in the inky blackness of the forest, she had no idea. Another of their capabilities? If it was all true, she could hardly wait for the initiation ceremony. She wondered where it would be held.

Canterra…he likened her to a beautiful flower on his planet. Heck, all she had ever known was ridicule. Her strange hair coloring especially had caused her to get teased a lot, specifically during her young schooling years. And her scales? Kids had shunned her because of her *disease*. But she finally knew it was not an affliction.

All the teasing and torturing she had endured had toughened her and conditioned her for her time as a cadet at the space academy. Her biggest fear had been that they would reject her, but she had passed all tests with such speed and flying colors, that they accepted her into the program.

Jasim stopped at the city border. She slid off his back.

"You will need to lead the way to your shop, Azilia."

"How did you know in which direction to run?"

"I scented your home. We absorb scents of where we have been and that stays with us. But now that I am in normal mode, you will need to lead."

"We will take some back streets. I am not sure if the authorities are watching the shop. Did you see the police flying below us?"

"Yes, I did. That is when I gained altitude, so they could not see us."

Snow began to fall in the city, too. They kept

close to buildings, and when they were on the corner of her street, Azilia peeked around the corner. "No one. It is safe I think."

"Maybe they have given up?"

"I hope so. I will not turn on the lights, just in case."

They swiftly darted into the shop. Azilia locked the door and groped for the flashlight where she had left it on the counter while working on the clock. She turned it on and led the way up the stairs.

Her tablet on the kitchen table pinged like crazy. Calls. Many. From her mother of course. She listened to the dozen or so messages.

After the last one, another persistent pinging sounded. She answered it, and her mother appeared in the holograph. It was evident she had been crying. "Zilly, are you all right? I have been worried out of my mind. We all are worried sick. The dragon—"

"Mother, I am fine, as you can see. Jasim is with me. He will not let anything happen to me."

"But young Tekelan saw a dragon. And when I raced outside, I saw it, too. Almost all of us did. And it had you in its claws."

"Mother, everything is fine. We just arrived home. You can inform the authorities that it was all a mistake, the overactive imagination of a young boy."

"I am not going to lie to them. I saw the beast with my own two eyes. You cannot tell me that it did not happen. How can you be fine after such an ordeal?"

"Tomorrow, Mother. Jasim and I will explain everything." Now Azilia had no choice. Her mother needed to know the truth of it all.

"You will both be here for breakfast?"

"Yes, we will. Goodnight, Mother. Say goodnight to the others for us?"

Jasim sank to a chair. "Will she call off the authorities?"

"I hope so. You heard me. I will have to tell her the complete truth now, even if it will break her heart." She let out a heavy sigh. "Would you like a cup of tea?"

"No, thank you. I would like to sleep for a few hours. Before we know it, morning will be here, and I heard your mother say we have to go to her home for breakfast. I do not think it a good idea to fly there."

Azilia giggled. "Eh, no. In broad daylight? I can imagine the uproar in the city if they spotted a dragon in the sky. Dragons are not real here on Pazona. We are taught they are mythological creatures, ones that children's stories are made up of, just like fairies and goblins. The people have to be made aware of your planet, and that it is largely inhabited by dragons. No, we cannot fly to the family estate. Although it has begun to snow, and that means low cloud cover. Actually, I think I will book a minicab now." She quickly logged in to the cab site and booked it for just before eight in the morning. That would give them enough time to shower and get ready.

"Did I tell you today how beautiful you look in that dress?"

"No, but you can tell me now." She felt the blood rising to her cheeks. *Oh, he can keep the compliments coming.* "Tomorrow I will just dress normally."

"Goodnight, canterra," he said, dropped a kiss on top of her head, and headed for his room.

Azilia took the mug of tea she had just made and went to her room. She discarded the dress, which had withstood the adventure remarkably well, took off her underwear, and crawled into bed. For a little while, she lay on her side sipping her tea until her eyelids finally felt too heavy. She set the half-finished tea on the nightstand, and within seconds she was off and away.

CHAPTER SIX

Azilia woke to the pinging of her tablet…again. It was her mother of course. "I thought I had better call you. It was very late last night. Do you need one of us to come and get you?"

"I ordered a minicab. We will be fine. Thanks, Mother."

We? Azilia knew it was all too real, but at times she still wondered if it was a ridiculous dream…until she heard Jasim going into the bathroom. She swung her legs out of bed and sat on the side for a few minutes. Her biggest ordeal was yet to come — telling her mother everything.

They should talk after breakfast, she decided, after most of the family had left. Time to explain to them could come later. And yes, she would have to tell the whole family.

Man, what a jar of pickles this has become. A favorite saying of her father's. Her father had brought some pickles back with him from Earth once, but neither she nor her mother and siblings had liked the strange tasting, big, green, fat worms in a jar.

She peeked to see if the coast was clear and scooted to the bathroom. After showering, then drying her hair, she went back to her room. Where Jasim was, she had no idea. Maybe in the kitchen?

Hurriedly she put on her suit, pulled on her boots, then headed for the kitchen. He was sitting on a chair looking through one of her grandmother's antique books that she had kept for herself. There were a lot of antique books in the shop. Some people were avid collectors and would pay a lot for a paper edition, especially if they were bound in leather.

"Good morning," she said as she filled the kettle, startling him.

"I did not hear you come in. This book is fascinating. All your grandmother's artifacts are, but the paper books interest me the most. It feels so different to read on paper rather than on a screen."

"We will have a quick cup of tea. I ordered the minicab for just before eight, so we will be on time for breakfast. I might add, a breakfast I am not looking forward to. This whole Christmas holiday has been just too weird."

He came up behind her and pushing her hair aside, kissed the nape of her neck. She leaned against him while she waited for the kettle to boil. She would need to get used to sharing her space with someone else—a man. That led her thoughts to her career. No way did she want to give it up, not yet. How was he going to react to that?

"I am sorry. I tried to block your thoughts, but when you are so quiet, I become curious. You wish to continue with your career, remain a chief engineer, and explore the galaxies. That would take you away from me for months on end. I cannot reconcile our betrothal with such long separations. Unless, we can get you a commission on my planet, or I can get one on yours, then we can explore the universe together."

It was true. But they had only just met. Sure, Azilia felt very strongly that he was the one, that she had waited her whole life for him. The tugging at the strings of her soul and heart was strong. But they hardly knew each other, and if she was going to be away a lot, how could they ever have a normal relationship?

"Canterra, your grandmother made it clear in her last wishes that she wants you to run her shop for two years. That means, unless you give up your inheritance, you cannot resume your career. The king and queen are far from ready to hand over the throne and go into retirement. I am quite willing to live here with you, as long as we travel back and forth between your planet and mine. That way we can learn everything there is to know about our worlds, and about each other."

She turned and gazed up at him. He was not joking. The expression in his eyes was earnest. "You would do that for me?"

"If I were able, I would merge our two worlds. I will do anything for you."

"Anything?"

He grinned down at her before bending and kissing her on the forehead. "Almost anything."

"We cannot just live together. It is unheard of that a man and woman live together before they wed. And it is too early to tie myself to you. What if we decide in a few months that we were not meant to be together after all?"

"Jantella always foretold you would be found, and that you and I would wed. One does not doubt Jantella's words."

"Jantella? Oh, right, your goddess sorceress. Quite amazing that she is a dragon, too."

"Yes, as we told you, there are quite a few of us. You have yet to meet my parents, and my two brothers and sister. Jantella is not just a goddess and sorceress, she is the most ancient dragon. She was the first and is very old."

"Mm, wonder where she originally came from. Or maybe she was some kind of organism that evolved?"

"I have never given it any thought. We have always accepted the fact that Jantella was the first and is the oldest of us all," Jasim said.

Azilia glanced at the clock on the wall. "We need to go. The minicab will be here shortly."

No sooner had she closed the shop door behind her and locked it, the cab arrived.

On the way to the estate, Azilia peered at Jasim. "It is strange. You have so often been in my dreams ever since I was young. I wonder if I have the gift of foresight."

"That was Jantella's magic. She explained it to me while you were talking with your true parents. The sorceress used her power to unite us in our dreams to help keep us connected. In a sense, we have known each other all of our lives."

She poked him. "Eh, I beg to differ. When I

arrived on your planet, I faced a dragon that scared the shit out of me. I never dreamed about dragons."

He chuckled, then leaned down and kissed her cheek. "We are here."

"Yes, and the interrogation squad awaits us." Azilia had said it in jest, but they were barely inside the house when they were bombarded with questions.

Azilia finally had enough. "Shut up, all of you! After breakfast, I am going to talk to Mother first. *Alone.* After that, Jasim and I will talk to you all. For now, let us go and enjoy a great breakfast together!" she shouted over the din.

Breakfast was already set out on the long dining table, a stack of plates at each end. Her mother came out of the kitchen with one last platter. She set it on the table and hugged Azilia. "After breakfast, Mother."

"I heard you. The neighbors probably did, too!"

Her mother had outdone herself. Platters piled with a mix of Earth and Pazonan foods stood on the table. Azilia had to explain many of them to Jasim, including what was an Earth recipe, and what was a home recipe.

No one mentioned anything during breakfast, though Azilia strongly felt the furtive glances in their direction and heard the soft whispers.

"Jasim, can you hear what they are saying?"

"No, canterra, I blocked my mind to their thoughts and whispers. When there are so many, it can get very busy in your head and give you a mighty headache." He pushed his plate away. "I am so full. I cannot eat anymore."

"Neither can I. Mother has gone back to the kitchen. We should go and talk to her now. If anyone else is in the kitchen, Mother will chase them out."

When they entered the kitchen and put their dirty plates in the sink, her mother closed the door and locked it.

"So…Zilly. You have much explaining to do." She crossed her arms over her bosom and frowned.

"Mother, I came prepared. I have a letter from Groma. I was not going to show this to anyone, but before we came here, I thought about it and felt you have the right to read it." She handed her mother her tablet that she had brought along at the last moment. Allowing her mother access to the document with her thumbprint, she stepped back and leaned against the counter and watched her mother's face while she read the letter.

When her mother finally finished and looked

up at Azilia, her eyes were brimming with tears about to spill. "How long were you going to keep this secret? The letter explains so much. My poor baby. I wonder what happened to her body when—"

"She is still alive, and her name is Tissara."

Her mother gasped. "But how? Where is she now?"

Azilia put both her arms around her mother's shoulders and hugged her hard. "You are, and always will be, my mother. I love you. Let me tell you the rest now, with Jasim's help, and then you can meet Tissara."

An hour later, Stabila was still wiping fat rolling tears off her face after they had told her everything.

"You are...are...a...dragon? A...princess?" her mother stammered.

"Yes, Mother. Apparently, I am such a beast, but I cannot shift until I have gone through some kind of initiation," Azilia said.

"You have to go back there?" Her mother's eyes grew big with fear.

"Mother, I will never ever, abandon you or my family. Please believe me? I love you, and my brothers and sisters. But you must understand how the queen feels? She lost her only child, and now that child has resurfaced. I will need to divide my time and loyalties between two families now. But my main loyalty will always remain with you and with Father. The two of you have made me what I have become." Azilia fought hard not to cry with her mother.

"How are we going to explain all this to the family?" her mother asked.

"The basics. Groma's letter is private. I will not share it with them. Jasim and I will also need to meet with the council to tell them about Jasim and his dragon. We do not want another incident like last night," Azilia said, patting her mother on the back.

"Perhaps in the future, the king and queen can travel through the portal and meet with your council to discuss diplomatic relations," Jasim suggested.

Her mother nodded. "Good idea, but please, I wish to meet Tissara now."

"Please wait here, Mother? I won't be long." Azilia stepped away from her mother and pictured the royal chambers in her mind, then drew a circle with her fingers.

Her mother gasped audibly and grabbed Azilia's arm. "Are you sure this is safe?"

"We will be just fine, Mother." Azilia took Jasim's hand, and they stepped through the portal she had created. Quick as a flash, the kitchen disappeared.

CHAPTER SEVEN

They had entered near the dining area in the royal quarters. Seated at the table were the king and queen, as well as Tissara and Jantella.

Tissara jumped from her seat. "You are back!"

"Only for a few moments." Azilia did not miss the instant look of disappointment on the king and queen's faces. "Mother wishes to meet Tissara. Please allow me some time to help my mother to adjust. I will be back soon. I promise."

"Of course, daughter. You have no idea how relieved we are that you have the ability to return to us," the king said. "Like you, we were wondering if it had all been a dream, but now we know it is so very real. I hope you are able to spend time with us very soon."

Tissara turned to Jantella. "Mother, you know I love you dearly, and I am grateful for the upbringing you gave me, but I have waited all of my life for this moment."

Jantella jumped up from her chair and hugged Tissara, her eyes wet with tears. "I wouldn't dream of keeping you away from your biological mother. Visit me often, for I shall miss you dearly."

"You know I will. Like Azilia, I must now divide my time between two families." Tissara joined Azilia and Jasim. "I am ready."

Azilia quickly opened the portal, and the three of them stepped through, the portal dissipating behind them. She noticed her head did not ache this time. Maybe she was getting used to this mode of travel.

Once again, they stood in her mother's kitchen. Stabila seemed rooted to the same spot Azilia had left her, a look of shock registering on her face.

Stabila's hands flew to her face. "You could be me when I was young."

Tissara rushed past Azilia and stopped short in front of her mother. "I have waited so long to finally meet you."

Stabila threw her arms around Tissara and drew her into a tight embrace. "You have your father's beautiful smile. If only he could have been here for this joyous event." Her eyes pooling, she drew back and motioned to Azilia to join them.

Azilia gazed at the tears streaming down her mother's cheeks. "Merry Christmas, Mother," she said and hugged them both.

"I am the luckiest mother." Stabila grasped both of their hands. "I have raised an incredible woman and gained a beautiful daughter." She smiled at Jasim. "And a future son. Now, let us go and tell the family about Tissara and the dragon. And after everyone has gone home, we need to talk more. We have a wedding to plan. I will not have the two of you living under one roof together."

"Mother, it is too soon. Jasim and I have barely met. We need to learn about each other first," Azilia told her.

"From what you have told me, it has been foretold. So, it will be. You can learn about each other after you are wed," her mother stubbornly said. "I will plan your wedding for a week from now."

Azilia knew there was no arguing with her mother. "Fine. How about we go and face the troops now?"

They tried to tell their tale the best they could and were bombarded with questions. The younger nephews and nieces were enthralled that their aunt and her soon to be husband were dragon shifters. The older ones were somewhat dubious. Azilia's brothers and sisters were hesitant, and not that forthcoming—though they were all enamored of Tissara. She had much of their mother's bubbly personality and looked more like her than any of them did.

Quentino drew Tissara into a hug. "Welcome to the family, sister."

Tissara smiled. "Thank you."

Azilia could see the joy on her face as their mother led Tissara around the room to meet the rest of their family.

Quentino peered at Azilia and Jasim. "As Father used to say, sounds like a pile of hogwash to me."

"Aw, Quent." Azilia referred to him by the nickname she had given him long ago. "Come on. Would I lie about this? I did not think it was real at first. But it is. Besides, you can see for yourself that Tissara is a true member of this family. Why would I lie about the dragons?"

"If you ever dare harm my little sister…" Quentino let the sentence trail off, but the threat was clear.

"You can wear my wedding dress," Jardana, her oldest sister, said suddenly.

"Or mine," Riatana, another sister offered.

"I think I would like to wear grandmother's wedding gown. I saw it in the closet. I think she would like that," Azilia decided.

For the next several hours, the chatter was all about weddings and wedding dresses and Tissara's life on Zuynus until most of her brothers and sisters decided it was time to leave.

"I am exhausted," Azilia rubbed her eyes. "It was a very late night, and today has been emotionally taxing. I am going home, too." She smiled at Tissara. "You are welcome to sleep at my place if you wish."

"If it is all right with Mother, I would love to stay here for the night," Tissara stated.

Stabila squeezed Tissara's shoulder. "I would like that very much."

Azilia smiled at them both. It had indeed become a joyous Christmas to see her mother brimming with happiness. The holiday had always been bittersweet since her father's passing. "She can stay in my old room." A yawn escaped her. "The minicab should be here." She said goodbye to her mother and Tissara and motioned for Jasim to follow her.

Her mother stopped him. "No, young man.

You will live here until your nuptials!"

Azilia laughed at Jasim's raised eyebrows. He looked at her for help, but Azilia knew there would be no arguing with her mother. "We are going to be very busy, Jasim. We need to bring the king and queen here to meet the family, and your family, too. We cannot have a wedding without them present."

Jasim nodded solemnly. "We must also join on my planet. There will be the traditional ceremony, but it will be extra special because it will include your initiation."

"Holy shit! That means transporting my complete family through the portal."

"And that expression means?" Jasim asked as he kissed her cheek.

"One of my father's. It is really quite meaningless but sounds good if I am shocked or astounded at something."

He gave her a quick hug, a kiss on the forehead, and a smile. "I love you, canterra. I will see you early tomorrow."

Chapter Eight

The day had finally arrived. It was only a week since Christmas, but it felt like a lifetime. Azilia saw Jasim almost every day, whenever she took time away from the shop, but when she went back in the evening, she felt empty and could hardly wait to see him again.

The evening before the wedding, she was not allowed to see him at all. *Bad luck*, the family told her.

Azilia twirled before the mirror in her mother's bedroom. The ceremony was going to be held in the great room of her parental home, which was now set up to hold at least a hundred guests. The family had decorated it with flower bouquets and floral garlands. Ribbons held a large net near the ceiling filled with white and mauve balloons. The first chair of each row of chairs had a floral spray attached to it. Azilia could hardly believe what her family had accomplished in such a short time.

The aroma of food wafted from the kitchen causing her stomach to growl. Azilia grimaced at her image, the sting in her eyes threatened tears at the deep-down wish her grandmother could be here on this special day.

Her grandmother's gown fit her to perfection. They might not be blood-related but had the same proportions. It was a beautiful satin and lace gown, slightly yellowed from age, making it a creamy color. The neckline scooped in a V to her breasts, showing just enough cleavage. Tiny sleeves covered her shoulders and the tops of her arms. The skirt hung in graceful folds from beneath her breasts and formed a long train at the back embroidered with lacy flowers. On her head, she wore the tiara her other mother had given her. Queen Mirra had told her it rightfully belonged to her as the crown princess.

Her mother came into the room wearing a smile. "Zilly, you look stunning. Heandra did a wonderful job with your hair."

Heandra was one of her oldest nieces who had become a hair stylist. She had worked on Azilia's hair for an hour before she was satisfied. It poufed a bit and was pulled up into loose curls resting on top of her head with a thick braid surrounding the cluster of curls. The tiara rested on the braid.

"I have your grandmother's necklace for you, Zilly. She left it to me, but I know she would be delighted to have you wear it today." Her mother showed her a string of beautiful pearls.

Azilia swallowed hard when her mother placed the pearls around her neck. She remembered them well because she had often played with them as a child.

"Can I just be alone for a little bit?" she said, looking at her mother.

"Sure, child. Just bang on the door when you are ready, but do not be too long. Jasim is anxiously waiting at the altar."

Azilia closed her eyes reliving everything from the moment the lawyer had given her the letter. Was it real? Would she wake up at any moment and find out it had, in reality, all been a silly dream?

"Stop it!" she told her reflection. "Jasim is waiting for you. Go get him, girl!"

And to think she would have to go through all this again when they wed on Zuynus. She squashed the thought and stood tall as she went to the door and opened it. Her mother handed her the spray of mauve and white flowers. Azilia walked slowly behind her mother to the top of the stairs, staying there until the music began. Slowly, she descended, and step by step walked toward her destiny.

"I thought it would never end," Jasim rained kisses from her forehead, down her nose, her neck, and her chest. He picked her up and deposited her on the big bed.

Without her knowledge, he had redecorated her grandmother's bedroom. He had painted it, cleaned it all out, rearranged it completely for the newlyweds to occupy. When he had done it all, she had no idea. *Maybe when I was busy in the shop?* He had lit a lot of candles. The scent combined with the heady perfume of the wedding flowers that had been moved to the room, made her feel dizzy. That and the wine she had consumed that evening. She vaguely wondered what he had done with her grandmother's things, but this was not the time to ask about them.

A silver bucket stood on the nightstand next to the bed, filled with ice and a bottle of wine. Two tall flutes stood next to it with a bow tied around the stems.

His fingers fumbled with all the tiny buttons on the back of the dress while she took everything in at a glance, but eventually, she felt the coolness of the room caress her skin. The warmth of his hand eased the chill as he peeled the dress down until she lay naked before him. Next, he removed the tiara and took the pins out of her hair until it tumbled in waves over the pillow.

Jumping off the bed, Jasim quickly took off his clothing and stood for a moment looking at her. She watched his eyes rake her body, rest on the V at the top of her thighs, hungrily access her breasts, before he fell on the bed beside her and stroked her tenderly.

"Canterra, my love, you take my breath away," he whispered as a hand closed over a breast, and his lips sought hers.

"I love you, my dragon," she whispered back and arched her hips.

"And to think we need to do this over again in a few days." He sighed.

"A few days?"

"Yes. What if you are with child after tonight? My sweet, tomorrow, we take our parents back to Zuynus and make the arrangements for our nuptials there."

"Pregnant? You are kidding me, right?" She punched him.

"This treatment of me is not effective on the night of our joining," he muttered.

"It might not be effective, but you better watch it. There is no way in hell I am ready to be a mother. I have far too much to do, too many places to see, too much to learn. Before I bear a child, I will and shall be a captain!"

"Aye, aye, sir." He gave her a mock salute.

"Do not make fun of me. I am very serious."

"And so am I. Be ready for me, my canterra. Spread your legs."

Azilia smiled demurely and let him fondle and kiss her. Deep within she knew what she wanted, and she was determined to get there. Little did Jasim know that she was well-schooled on the methods of how to prevent pregnancy.

All thoughts of children, pregnancy, and captaining a ship flew from her mind when he leaned forward and captured her lips. Her body on fire, she spread her legs, and as he gained entry to that unexplored territory, she knew she had finally come home. She had found her roots, her future, and she had a man who would always stand by her.

Other books by Taryn and Gabby:

In Search of Pride

The gods smile upon a weary warrior...

Brenn, a warrior returning home from battle, rests by a tempting magical pool and meets a siren who changes his life forever.

Bound by a curse, he must find a way to save his pride.

He returns from a war far from his home to find that his village is destroyed and his pride missing. With the help of his guardian dragon, Ciara, he sets out to find his missing family and pride.

After Ciara saves Brenn's life twice, he begins to realize that he is not as invincible as he once thought. He must accept his limitations and the help of his lifemate to keep him safe.

Excerpt:

There are morcougs nearby. They have scented the blood of the deceased that are still on the ship. The bodies must be taken care of right away. Ciara's warning was loud and clear in his mind.

"Erica, there is danger nearby. Warn your crew to return to the ship."

"Really? How do you know? I do not hear or see anything," she responded.

Just after she spoke, Ciara swooped down.

The crew vaulted up and panicked, several of the female crewmembers screaming and running back to the ship. Erica and her first officer drew their weapons and were ready to fire.

Brenn, Laro, and Ivran jumped up and reached for their weapons.

"What are you doing? Stop. I can disintegrate this beast in a second," Erica shouted.

The noise was unbelievable. Men and women yelling, some screaming, many reaching for their weapons. "Erica, this dragon is friendly. She is here to protect us. Just watch," Laro told her.

Hesitantly, Erica lowered her arm a bit, though not sheathing her weapon. In seconds, Ciara breathed fire into the nearby shrubs and trees, and two roaring morcougs came stumbling out, their fur in flames. Again, Ciara blew fire at them, and they were incinerated within a minute.

Ciara flapped her wings and soared into the sky.

"Now I've seen everything," Erica said and sheathed her weapon. "Dragons on Earth occur only in stories and legends."

"The dragon will watch over us. I advise you to tell your people to bed down for the night, and you and your officer should do the same," Brenn said.

Tabeka's Revenge
Book 8
Crimson Realm Chronicles

A heart betrayed… A soul crushed… Plotting revenge never felt so sickly sweet…

Ignoring her mother's warnings, Tabeka forms a relationship with Lord Cidus Milhella, the man chosen for her by the gods as shown her by the goddess Rania. However, her vision does not prepare her for the terrible price she must pay.

Betrayed by Cidus, disowned by her father and abandoned, Tabeka forges a life alone in the forests of Wildevein.

Years later, Cidus seeks Tabeka's healing assistance to help his mate birth him a healthy heir. His request plants the seed for a plan of vengeance in Tabeka's heart—one that will destroy Cidus and his goal for Wildevein.

Excerpt

It was almost dawn when Tabeka hurried home, carrying her precious bundle in a cloth bag. Ivia had delivered that night, but nothing Tabeka did, or the herbs and potions she had fed the woman, had stopped the bleeding. Ivia had passed on to the realm of dreams shortly after the birth of the feeble girl child. The infant had cried. Not a lusty wail as it should have been, but a soft mewling sound. Nevertheless, Tabeka had given her a few drops of sleep elixir. She could not chance Cidus hearing the child.

Earlier that night, she had brought the boy that Vilore had delivered a few days before, to the manor the same way — wrapped up well and hidden in the cloth bag, sleeping soundly from the elixir. He was a beautiful infant, healthy, and had a lusty cry.

Vilore had come to Tabeka's shack three days before to deliver him there to avoid questions from her older children and others and had left, happy with her bag of gold. She had told Tabeka she would tell neighbors and friends the infant had died at birth. And she was taking her children the next day and moving to another realm to start a new life.

For three days Tabeka had cared for the boy, in between visits to the manor, until a servant came banging on her door in the middle of the night to tell her that Ivia's time to deliver had come.

Cidus had not seemed to care that his mate was gone. He was only interested in the boy child and charged a servant to find a wet-nurse in the village. "I will call him Evior," he had told Tabeka. "I am in your debt, and if you will weave your magick to make sure the boy reaches maturity, you will receive a bag of gold every year from this day forth until he has seen twenty-five summers." He had handed her a large bag of gold.

Once inside her shack, Tabeka threw the bag of gold on the table and took the tiny girl out of the bag. She still slept but breathed normally. "Your name will be Iridia," she whispered as she held the infant against her. "I will give you a good life, little one."

Unwrapping the old blanket, she carefully washed the baby, then dressed her in the clothing she had bought over the last months and swaddled her in a new, soft, blanket. She was so tiny, it worried Tabeka. Now that she had a daughter to care for, she would use Cidus' gold to buy land and have the local carpenter build a cottage not too far from the village, and she would raise her properly. No one would ask questions. The type of clothing she wore could have hidden a swelling belly easily. And the villagers liked her services so would not question her.

She sang softly and rocked the infant, gazing into her now open eyes and stroking her downy black hair. She promised to be a pretty little girl. Then again, Ivia was a beautiful woman with her long black hair, brown eyes and heart-shaped face.

"You are my daughter." Tabeka rested her cheek against the tuft of hair. Her vengeance was almost complete, but it would take quite a few years for her revenge to come to its final conclusion.

Books in the Crimson Realm Chronicles:

In Search of Pride – Book 1

The Dragon's Lion – Book 2

Sword of Betrayal – Book 3

Sword of Judgement – Book 4

Testing the Crown – Book 5

Shard in the Mirror – Book 6

Initiation Genesis – Book 7

Tabeka's Revenge – Book 8

Infinite Fury – Book 9 – Coming Soon

Related to this series:

The Lion's Stowaway
The Frozen Portal

The Lion's Stowaway

A novella based on the Ierilian world of the Crimson Realm Chronicles and its characters, published in an anthology with Viola Grace and other authors. Buy it at extasybooks.com and please help to support the authors by purchasing directly from the publisher!

Sometimes what you know to be the truth is nothing but an elaborate lie.

Azilia's life is turned upside down when her grandmother leaves her an old antique shop in her will, forcing her to run the musty old store for two years or lose her inheritance.

Reluctant to accept her inheritance, she is given a letter written by her grandmother that changes the stakes—and Azilia's life forever.

Excerpt:

Heading back on the familiar trail, that she could almost walk blindfolded now, she hummed a tune. That was something she missed. Music.

When she was close to her tree, a sound startled her. It was too loud to be made by one of the little furry creatures she so often saw darting around among the flowers. She stopped. Her heart sped up. She'd seen no other human in the forest since she'd lived there. Not once. The sound came from the direction of the crate.

Standing very still, she held her breath and waited. A crack, then another. Suddenly a huge lion faced her. She dropped her basket, her purchases spilling to the forest floor, screamed, and ran to the nearest tree.

She peeked at the lion from behind the trunk and started hitching up her skirts to tie them in a knot above her knees. "Go away, kitty!"

She hoisted herself onto a branch and started climbing. When she was halfway up the tree, she dared to look down. She couldn't remember. Did lions climb?

"Nice kitty, kitty, kitty." She climbed a couple more limbs but dared not go any higher. The branches were starting to get thin and might break beneath her weight. She leaned forward and peered down at the lion.

"Holy shit! You are one big cat!"

He was the biggest lion she'd ever seen. Their parents had taken them to a zoo when she and Hannah were still little. The lions had awed her and had seemed gigantic. But this one was huge. Of course, he had to be. It was an alien lion.

What in the hell was she going to do? Was it hungry? Was it looking at her for its next meal? She grabbed the piece of smoked meat she had in her pocket, pulled a chunk off it with her teeth and held her hand out. "Look, kitty. Mmm, it's good, see?"

She threw the piece of meat. It landed on the ground a distance from the tree. "Go get it, boy!"

The lion just stood looking up at her. He did not attempt to climb or approach the tree...nor did he go after the food. To her consternation, he suddenly growled. Then it appeared as if his bones were popping through his skin.

"Oh, fuck, no!"

It freaked her the hell out. It was like the movie *Thing*. An alien made itself look like a dog, but when it showed its true form, it was a grotesque monster.

She couldn't take her eyes away. It was all so crazy. It wasn't a hideous creature he was mutating into. When the transformation was complete, he had become the most gorgeous hunk of male flesh she'd ever seen. She rubbed her eyes and looked again. Was she going insane? *Okay… I'm dreaming. There is no way this is real.* She pinched herself. *Wake up, Izzy.*

VEILED ELIMINATORS SERIES

EXTRICATION

VEILED ELIMINATORS 1

eX

GABRIELLA
BRADLEY

TARYN
JAMESON

RECREANCY

VEILED ELIMINATORS 3

(eX)

GABRIELLA
BRADLEY

TARYN
JAMESON

About the Authors

Taryn Jameson is a mother, artist, and avid reader who lives in an enchanted forest that sparks her imagination to create. Her latest outlet is the written word. She is the alter ego of cover artist Angela Waters.

Gabriella Bradley has been a writer and artist all her life, though only ventured into erotic works in 2003. Her hobbies include hiking, gardening, swimming, sewing, embroidery. Favorite movies are old timers like Gone with the Wind, Spartacus, etc. Favorite TV series: Fringe. Favorite music is Abba.